D1483671

ISBN: 978-1-9992336-7-9 (e-book)
ISBN: 978-1-9992336-4-8 (Paperback)

This book is a work of fiction. Names, characters, and places are products of the author's imagination or are used fictitiously, and any resemblance to actual persons, living or dead, events, business establishments or locales is entirely coincidental.

Cover image by Bobooks.

First edition 2020.

To the SkyTalons flock.
Thank you for flying with me on this adventure!

# SKYTALONS

## SHADOWS WITHIN

# PROLOGUE

*Many years ago...*

Khan was pretty sure he had made some good distance between himself and the horrifically huge creature behind him. It was hard to tell when running for your life.

It had only been a couple of seconds ago when life finally seemed to be going his way. Khan had been made a Speaker at last, had starry-eyed fantasies of Jarquanzila, his biggest hero, coming to personally greet him, and being a legend among the five tribes (although he hadn't quite worked out the details of that last one yet).

But now here he was, nearly tripping over his own feet to avoid a gigantic, scaly yellow talon. Khan gasped as it came rushing toward him, each claw dangerously extended. He jumped to the side, narrowly missing the talon by only a wing's length. He felt a few of his feathers get torn from his side, but he barely noticed. Khan felt nothing but fear surging through his veins.

The peacock-sized claw retreated for a moment, rearing up for its next attack.

"Jarquanzila? Why are you doing this? Wh-what did I do?!" Khan spluttered, out of breath. His gaze darted back and forth, searching for some way out of this awful void of nothingness.

He felt a flash of fear.

There was no sign of safety up ahead. Khan could feel his energy draining. If he couldn't find some means of escape soon, he might never get to see his family or tribe again. *No, I've come too far!* Khan thought, forcing himself to move faster. *I can't give up now. Think, Khan, think! There has to be another way out of here.* Khan forced himself to look behind him, then felt his blood run cold. He found himself gazing into the furious, green eyes of Jarquanzila himself.

Suddenly, Khan felt something inside of him snap. Panic and terror gripped him so fiercely that he came to an abrupt halt. Khan turned around to face Jarquanzila. He felt his talons tremble. "You... you're a monster," Khan whispered.

Jarquanzila let out a dangerous screech, taking a step forward.

Anger swept through Khan, his feathers beginning to flare. He held Jarquanzila's gaze challengingly. "You've lied to us all, haven't you!" he screamed. "You don't actually care about the tribes. You don't care about anything or anyone but *yourself*!"

Jarquanzila's eyes narrowed into two cold slits. "The tribes mean more to me than you'll ever know," he softly growled. "And that is why I cannot, and will not, have you interfere with my plans." Jarquanzila lifted a massive talon. Then, in a flash, he launched it toward him. Khan braced himself, sure that this was the end.

Just as it was about to collide with him, Khan felt an icy grip on his shoulder, and he was pulled backward. The last thing he saw was Jarquanzila's talon just a second away from him, and the shadowy black claws of his rescuer.

With a gasp, Khan lifted his head from the sandy ground inside of the Life Tree, finding himself back in the Peacock Tribe.

"I... I had been so terrified," Khan confessed, forcing his voice not to shake. Even though this story had happened long ago, when he was just barely older than a hatchling, it still pained him as if it had happened yesterday. "I went to tell my father, Thargus, everything that had happened," Khan continued. "But he dismissed me, telling me that I had dreamt the whole thing up." His beak clenched. "No bird believed me. Everyone thought I was crazy. So I told myself that if they weren't going to listen to me, I would *make* them listen."

Khan, even after all this time, still couldn't help but feel proud of what he had done. "I destroyed as many branches of the Life Tree that I could, before some bird stopped me. I did it right in the middle of the day, with everyone there to see it," he said. "I told the tribe that I would be the one to save them all, no matter the cost. Jarquanzila will be destroyed, and they can either be with me, or against me." Khan smirked, remembering how powerful he had felt in that moment.

"It was then that some of the tribe began to wake up. They had realized the truth about Jarquanzila," Khan continued. "After my own father exiled me, they followed me into banishment. Little did Thargus know that in that moment, he had launched my rebellion against Jarquanzila, and the start of the rogues."

Khan pushed his memories away, then turned to face his companion. "We *must* destroy Jarquanzila," he told the peacock.

"Because if we don't, the same thing that happened to me will happen to every other bird."

Khan felt his feathers bristle. *If only the tribes knew the danger coming their way,* he thought darkly. *I wish they would understand that I only want to help them. But it doesn't matter. One day I know they'll remember me as the hero of this story, not the cold-hearted villain.*

Khan felt sick as he silently looked up at the sunrise. He hated the monster he had become. He hated his terrible actions. And, most of all, he hated what he still needed to do.

"Something's troubling you?" his companion asked, speaking for the first time since meeting with Khan on top of Misty Falls.

Khan hadn't realized until now that he had been digging his talons into the dirt. Khan offered a small nod.

Every one of his companion's feathers were outlined in a brilliant red as the rising sun crept slowly above the jungle's trees. A chilly wind tore through the two rogue's feathers, and the trees behind them began to sway.

Khan thought carefully about his next words. Without warning, awful memories began to slither into his thoughts.

Khan remembered what he had done to Zander. He remembered the terror on the faces of every bird that saw him, including his own allies. Khan remembered Thargus, his own father, who was gone now because of him.

Guilt hit Khan so fiercely that he almost staggered backward. *It had to be done,* he told himself. Khan froze, terrified, feeling his heartbeat quicken. *Right?*

Ever since the last battle with the Peacock Tribe, Khan, for the first time in a very long time, had begun to question his choices. Khan couldn't shake the ghastly feeling that all of this pain, all of this suffering, all of this fear, had been for nothing. Every time he tried to push his doubts away, the stronger they latched onto him.

*Was I wrong about what I saw that night? Was I wrong about everything?* Khan warily asked himself. Anger shot through him. *No, I'm right. I know that I'm right. I have to be.*

He could feel his companion's gaze burn into his dark plumage. Khan felt a flash of gratitude toward the peacock. This was the only bird that Khan trusted right now, even more than himself.

Khan could feel himself growing softer by the day. He knew that Ellagard was the Peacock Tribe's new leader now. And because of this, she had become Khan's biggest enemy.

Would he be prepared to end her life like he had done to Thargus? Would he be able to kill any of his former tribemates again? Khan stared at his talons for a very long moment. *No,* he answered himself at last. *No, I wouldn't. This is between me and Jarquanzila!*

Without warning, a powerful emotion struck Khan. It was fast, and he almost mistook it as his own. Before he could stop himself, he let out a laugh. Khan's old confident, doubtless self suddenly came rushing back to him.

Khan's companion blinked at him. "Is it time?" they asked.

"Oh yes," Khan responded, feeling a grin slide over his face. "It *is* time. And soon, we will destroy Jarquanzila from the inside. We are going to end this war, once and for all!"

# CHAPTER 1

"I'm glad that I have gotten all of you together at last," said Jarquanzila. "Because now it is time to begin the next phase of your mission."

Cornelius felt nervousness grip him as he took in the nothingness of Jajarii. He instinctively moved closer to Shadow, feeling comforted when his feathers brushed against hers. Cornelius turned his attention to the small blue jay, who stood shyly in front of his fellow SkyTalons. When his blue eyes met with Cornelius', he offered an awkward grin.

"H-hello, SkyTalons," the flustered blue jay began, bowing his head. "I'm really pleased to meet you both. My name is Dustin and I-"

"Dustin, that was your memory, wasn't it? What had happened?" Shadow asked, cutting him off. The raven's tone was sharper than she had meant it to be. "Who were those birds, and why were they attacking your tribe?"

Cornelius flinched, remembering Dustin's terrifying memory. *The whole tribe was fleeing and scared. There was something, or someone, coming for them,* he thought with a gulp. Cornelius looked at Dustin, who had dropped his gaze and was now studying his talons. *I feel bad for Dustin. It seems like he was really looking forward to meeting us. But Shadow's right to be worried. There's something terribly wrong within the Blue Jay Tribe, and we need to find out what it is.*

Dustin hesitated for a moment. "There's some neighbouring birds that are looking for a fight," he confessed. More optimistically he added, "But they shouldn't be a problem now that we're all together."

Shadow and Cornelius exchanged an unconvinced look. *I have a feeling that it won't be that easy,* Cornelius thought grimly.

Shadow, smoothing her feathers, nodded encouragingly to Dustin. "Can you tell us more about these birds? Who are they? When did they start attacking?" she gently asked.

Dustin opened his beak to respond. Just as he was about to speak, Jarquanzila let out an annoyed screech.

"Silence, all of you!" he hissed. "We don't have much time left. The more I look into the future, the darker the tribe's path becomes. There is a terrible shadow rising within, a new kind of threat that I, nor the tribes, have ever seen before. It must be stopped right away, or else all will be lost."

Cornelius felt his heart pound, dread washing over his feathers. *We came to the Blue Jay Tribe looking for safety,* he remembered. *But now it looks like we've come to the most dangerous place of all.*

To Cornelius' shock, Dustin looked as though he was trying to stifle a laugh. "Trust me," Dustin began nonchalantly. "It isn't as bad as you all think. The tribe is perfectly safe, and we have everything under control. The only thing that those birds want is more territory, not the destruction of the whole tribe or anything. And now that the three of us are together, there's even less to worry about. We'll sort this out, no problem."

Cornelius shifted uncomfortably, far from feeling reassured. *Those birds... they seem far more dangerous than Dustin thinks that they are,* he reflected. *I can just feel it.*

Shadow lifted her head. "Jarquanzila? What should we do now?" she asked. "How can we stop these birds?" Her words were met by a chilling silence.

"Jarquanzila?" Shadow repeated.

Silence.

Dustin and Cornelius exchanged a worried glance. *Something isn't right,* he realized. Cornelius found himself taking a protective step closer to Shadow and Dustin, his talons extended.

Without warning, the world around them began to violently rumble. Cornelius gasped, terrified, as he almost lost his balance.

CRACK!

The three SkyTalons jumped backward as the black floor of Jajarii seemed to tear into two right in front of them, almost swallowing them up. With a terrible groan, the gorge began to expand, rushing toward the three SkyTalons at a startling speed. Cornelius and Shadow both threw open their wings, ready to fly for their lives.

Just as Cornelius was about to take off, he caught sight of Dustin. The young blue jay stood motionlessly, frozen with fear. His blue feathers were spiked out in panic.

The gorge was almost upon them now. Cornelius rushed forward. He quickly clamped his beak on the back of Dustin's neck feathers and pulled him backward.

Dustin, finally breaking out of his shock, launched into the air. Cornelius quickly followed him, and together they both flew in beside Shadow.

"What do we do?!" Cornelius screamed over the noise of the void. Jajarii was still violently rumbling. As the three SkyTalons flew, more and more cracks appeared in the void.

Shadow's eyes were round with fear. "I don't know!" she exclaimed. "Where is Jarquanzila? He needs to help us!"

"Oh my, you have so much trust in that bird," said a new icy, chilling voice. Cornelius flinched as a slow laugh slithered through his ears. "What a mistake. Jarquanzila won't help you now..."

The rumbling of the void abruptly stopped. The three SkyTalons pulled themselves into a hover, turning toward the direction of the voice. Cornelius let out a gasp of surprise.

Within the gorge that had almost swallowed Dustin was a shape. As Cornelius studied it more carefully, he recognized the features of a bird. *But it looks so... strange,* Cornelius reflected, suddenly feeling queasy.

The bird was shadow-like, as though the darkness of Jajarii had been liquefied and dumped onto their plumage.

Without warning, the bird's head shot up. Heavy globs, that could only be described as inky shadows, dripped down their feathers. The strange goo masked the bird's identity.

Cornelius recoiled as the bird lifted a talon and hooked it on the edge of the gorge. With a grunt, the shadow pulled itself out, then looked up. Their black, beady eyes studied each SkyTalon in turn. Cornelius felt a stab of terror as the shadow's gaze crawled over him. A lifetime seemed to pass. Then, in a flash, the shadow flung open their wings and rushed toward the three SkyTalons.

9

Cornelius gasped as their black, extended talons aimed straight for Shadow. *No!* he thought, horrified. Without thinking, Cornelius darted to the side, putting himself between Shadow and the horrific creature.

Hot pain shot through him as the shadow roughly clawed him aside. Cornelius felt the breath get knocked from out of his chest as he lost his balance and began to plummet.

"No, no, no!" Dustin gasped. For a moment, he watched, torn, as one of his fellow SkyTalons plummeted to the floor of Jajarii, while the other fought viciously with their attacker.

*Help Shadow, please!* Cornelius wordlessly pleaded, nearing the ground. In a blur of blue feathers, Dustin half-folded his wings and sped toward Cornelius. *No!*

Dustin crashed into Cornelius' side, knocking him back into balance. Cornelius quickly recovered, then looked up, searching for Shadow. Dread, fear, and anger surged through him. She was nowhere to be seen. Shadow, and their attacker, were gone.

Cornelius felt dizzy. "Shadow, no," he whispered.

Dustin blinked, confused, before following his gaze up to the inky sky of Jajarii. "I... I'm so sorry," Dustin whimpered as Cornelius sunk to the floor. His eyes sparkled with guilt as he landed beside him. "I didn't think that-"

"Don't ever put me before Shadow!" Cornelius screamed, his emotions getting the better of him. Dustin flinched. "Don't ever risk her safety for me, not *ever*! Shadow means the world to me, and now she's gone." He buried his head in his wings.

Dustin was at a loss for words. Silence gripped the void.

*Shadow was everything to me, and it's my fault that she's gone. How am I going to save the tribes without her? How am I going to do anything without her?* Cornelius wondered, feeling hollow with sadness.

Without warning, Dustin let out a gasp. He sprang forward, flying over Cornelius' head. Cornelius whirled around.

The shadow was back!

Cornelius recoiled as the creature's lifted talon shot forward, ready to tear him to shreds. Just before the shadow could strike, Dustin collided into them. A sickening grin appeared on the shadow's face. The bird raised a massive talon and slammed it into Dustin. The small blue jay was sent crashing to the ground with a sickening thud.

Fear gripped Cornelius.

"No!" Dustin gasped as the shadow began to prowl toward Cornelius.

Cornelius tried to get up, then flinched with pain, crumpling back to the ground. He forced himself to lift his head and extend his talons. *I have to be brave for Dustin,* Cornelius told himself, meeting the black, empty stare of the shadow. But right now, Cornelius felt anything but brave. His heart was pounding and his wings were trembling.

Without warning, the shadow sprang. Cornelius slammed his eyes shut, flinching.

A furious screech abruptly tore through Jajarii. He gasped, opening his eyes. Cornelius watched, frozen with fear, as the blinding, glowing white shape of Jarquanzila pelted the shadow with swipe after swipe from his talons.

*He's driving the shadow back,* Cornelius realized, dizzy with relief. *We're saved!*

Cornelius rushed forward to Dustin's side and nudged him with a talon. "We have to go," he urged. "Can you fly?"

Dustin didn't seem to hear. He was watching, transfixed, as the shadow and Jarquanzila viciously fought with beak and talon.

In a flash, the shadow collided with Jarquanzila, sending him tumbling backward. They let out a laugh. "Oh, *finally,*" the shadow sneered. "I've been waiting for this for far too long!" They sprang forward with a dangerous screech, each of their black talons extended.

Jarquanzila waited until the shadow was just a feather's length away from him before clamping his beak around one of their legs. With all of his strength, Jarquanzila roughly slammed the shadow against the floor of Jajarii. The whole void seemed to rumble with the force of the blow.

The shadow laid there for a moment, stunned, their breath coming in sharp wheezes.

Jarquanzila's green eyes hurriedly scanned the void until they rested on the two SkyTalons. Cornelius watched, mesmerized, as Jarquanzila closed his eyes and lifted a wing, pointing it forward into the depths of Jajarii. Within moments, a spot in the blackness seemed to melt away, revealing a forest on the other side. Jarquanzila's eyes snapped open. "Go," he ordered, turning his back on them. "I can only hold it open for so long!"

Jarquanzila, who was now the only one standing between the two SkyTalons and the shadow, braced himself for another attack.

Cornelius forced himself to peel his gaze away, turning it onto Dustin. He quickly helped him get up before unfurling his wings. Within moments, the two SkyTalons were flying for their lives, heading toward the rift in the void.

The shadow let out a furious hiss. They exploded forward, just barely missing an intercepting blow from Jarquanzila, and began to fly. Cornelius gasped as the shadow advanced on them, getting closer and closer by the second.

The rift—and safety—was almost within their reach. *We're not going to make it!* Cornelius realized. Dustin was beginning to trail behind, his energy draining. *No, no, no!*

Dustin's eyes were wide with panic as they darted to the rift and Cornelius in front of him, and then to the shadow just a wing's length behind him. For a moment, Dustin closed his eyes and let out a sigh. Then, with a sudden burst of speed, he thundered forward.

Cornelius gasped as Dustin crashed into him, pushing him forward. Cornelius blinked, then found himself on the other side of the rift. He was safe!

But Dustin wasn't.

"Come on!" Cornelius called. "You're almost there!"

The shadow loomed over Dustin now.

Just as Dustin was about to fly through the rift, the shadow extended a talon, snagging it around the small blue jay. Dustin was pulled backward.

"Cornelius!" Dustin cried.

Cornelius felt fear surge through him. He rushed forward to help. But, just before he could reach Dustin and the shadow, the rift closed, sealing them both inside. "No!" Cornelius screamed.

Dustin was gone.

Cornelius had now lost two SkyTalons.

# CHAPTER 2

Cornelius gasped with disbelief. Horror made him feel light. "No!" was all Cornelius managed to choke out.

Even though he knew it was hopeless, he flew forward to where the rift had been, desperately trying to find some way back inside Jajarii. He tried entering again, and again, and again, but to no prevail.

Cornelius let out a small whimper, the realization striking him like frozen talons. *Dustin and Shadow are gone, and it's all my fault,* he thought emptily.

*My fault, my fault, my...* the words kept on repeating in his head as he blindly sunk to the closest branch on the lush forest below. Cornelius pulled himself into a small ball with his wings, feeling his tears beginning to flow.

Rain began to fall from the grey sky above, soaking Cornelius' plumage. Wind blew past the trees, whispering as it went, almost as though it was mocking Cornelius.

*How could I have let this happen? How could I have lost the only hope for the tribes?* he asked himself, feeling guilt latch its countless, sharp talons around his heart. *How could I have been such a failure?*

"Cornelius?" a faraway voice abruptly called. It echoed through the vast forest, just barely managing to make its way to him.

Cornelius blearily lifted his head, wiping away his tears with a wing. "Hello?" he warily called out. Instinctively, he extended his talons, preparing himself for the first signs of danger. "Hello?" he repeated, more loudly this time.

"Cornelius?" the voice called again, this time sounding closer. He blinked, scanning the forest. The sound of flapping wings emerged from the silence. Cornelius whirled around. Then, he let out a gasp, feeling joy flood through him.

"Shadow!" Cornelius called, dizzy with relief.

The large, dark shape of Shadow emerged from the cover of the many trees. The moment she caught sight of Cornelius, her eyes sparkled with happiness. Shadow swooped down and perched close beside him.

Cornelius felt his heart pound, emotions flashing through him. "Shadow, you're okay! I-I never thought... I didn't think..." he rambled. Just as he was about to wrap his wings around her in a hug, he quickly thought the better of it and stopped himself. *I don't know if she feels the same way about me yet,* he told himself.

"How did you escape?" Cornelius hurriedly asked Shadow. "The last I saw of you, that... monster was attacking you. And then you disappeared and I-"

Shadow let out a heavy sigh. For the first time, Cornelius noticed how shaken she looked. Her midnight-black feathers were ruffled, and her eyes were glazed with concern. "Cornelius," Shadow began, her gaze locking with his, "I didn't think that I was going to make it out of there. If Jarquanzila didn't come and save me when he did, I don't think that I would be here right now."

Cornelius gasped, a fresh wave of guilt hitting him.

Suddenly, a thought struck him. "No," he began, thinking out loud. "But if you made it out, and Jarquanzila helped you, then Dustin must have escaped as well!"

Shadow blinked in confusion. "Cornelius, what are you talking about?" she slowly asked, her voice hoarse. "Where is Dustin? He's here with you, isn't he?"

Cornelius took a step backward, feeling his feathers begin to ruffle. The fear in his eyes must have said it all.

Shadow let out a gasp, recoiling slightly. "Cornelius, please don't tell me it's true. Dustin escaped, right? Please tell me he escaped!" she demanded.

A lifetime seemed to pass before Cornelius slowly shook his head. Shadow blinked in disbelief, then turned her head and looked away from him. A few silent seconds passed before Shadow spoke again.

"It isn't your fault, Cornelius," she gently murmured. "Please don't blame yourself."

Cornelius felt something inside of him snap.

"I do blame myself, and it is my fault!" he yelled, his stress getting the better of him. "If I wasn't plummeting to the ground and being *useless*, then you would have still been there, and *Dustin wouldn't be gone now*," he ended in a whimper.

Shadow was silent for a very long time. "What do we do now?" she asked at last.

Cornelius turned around, refusing to let her see him cry. *I don't know what we should do,* he thought. *The whole reason for coming to the Blue Jay Tribe was to unite with Dustin, and after that we were supposed to save the Peacock Tribe. But without three SkyTalons, is there any point in trying anymore?*

For a moment, Cornelius' thoughts flashed back to Donovan, his grandfather and one of the previous three SkyTalons before him. *Will Jarquanzila just replace us with other birds to be SkyTalons, like he replaced Donovan with me?* Cornelius wondered. *Will my curse of being a SkyTalon be passed on to my siblings, Jemma or Xavier? Or how about one of their hatchlings?* Cornelius shook his head, as if doing so would clear the thought. He couldn't think about that now.

"We should do what Dustin would have wanted us to do," Cornelius answered Shadow at last. "We should continue our mission. We'll go to the Blue Jay Tribe, and save them from the Shadow Within."

Shadow didn't respond. Silence gripped the forest. Cornelius blinked. "Shadow?" he asked, turning around. He let out a gasp.

Standing where Shadow would have been was a tall, slender blue jay. Her calculating, green eyes studied Cornelius carefully as she dug her talons in and out of the soft bark underfoot. Her feathers were smooth and relaxed as she waited for Cornelius to make the first move.

Cornelius froze. Suddenly, anger burned beneath his plumage. It was so fierce that Cornelius felt surprised with himself. But right now, he didn't care. Cornelius had thought that he had lost Shadow once already, and he wasn't about to lose her again! "Where is she?" he demanded. "If you touched even a single one of her feathers-"

"She's fine," the blue jay replied flatly. "But that can easily change, depending on what you do next." She took a step forward, her icy gaze locked on Cornelius. Slowly, she extended her talons. "Who are you?" she demanded. "And why are you on our land?"

Cornelius blinked. *On their land?* he wondered. *They must be from the Blue Jay Tribe! We did it, we finally made it!*

Cornelius relaxed his talons and smoothed his feathers. The blue jay watched him carefully, keeping her guard up.

"It's okay, there's no need to fight," he explained. "My name is Cornelius, and my companion is Shadow of the Raven Tribe. We were sent here by Jarquanzila, and we only want to help your tribe."

The blue jay stared at him for a long moment, her piercing gaze unwavering. After a few terribly long seconds, the blue jay did a quick flick of her tail feathers. The clusters of leaves around Cornelius suddenly came to life as a talonful of blue jays slunk out of them, joining him and the first blue jay on the branch.

Cornelius looked around nervously for Shadow. After a few seconds she, while being closely flanked by two other blue jays, joined him on the branch.

The first blue jay reluctantly relaxed her talons and smoothed her plumage. "You two are the SkyTalons, I presume?" she softly growled. "What an *honour* it is to meet you both." Her beak clenched.

Shadow dipped her head respectfully. "You must be Commander Myra, head of your tribe's Protectors," she greeted. "My cousin, Aquila, had always spoken highly of you."

Although the rest of the blue jays missed it, Cornelius saw the flash of sadness in Shadow's eyes when she spoke about her cousin.

Cornelius flinched, remembering how hard it had been on Shadow after the avalanche had fallen on Aquila and the other ravens back in the mountains. *I thought that Shadow had moved past her grief,* Cornelius thought with a frown. *I guess she's better at hiding her emotions than I thought.*

Myra offered a slow nod. "Our Speaker, Dustin, has been foretelling your arrival for days now, but we couldn't be sure of who you were until after we've spoken with you. I apologize for introducing ourselves like this. We have been having some... issues... with neighbouring birds," she said.

Shadow and Myra locked gazes for a long time. Finally, Myra looked away, turning her attention on to a small blue jay who stood nervously amongst the others.

"Alessandra," Myra snapped. The small blue jay took a step forward, watching Myra with anticipation. "Fly ahead and tell the tribe that the SkyTalons are coming."

Alessandra nodded before swooping off the branch and into the stormy sky beyond. Myra watched her go before turning to Shadow and Cornelius. "Come with us," she said before turning around and unfolding her wings.

Cornelius felt terror curl its long talons around his heart as he and the patrol took off. Soon, his racing heart matched the fast-paced drumming of the cold rain. *We're about to enter a whole new tribe... a whole new world,* Cornelius thought, feeling sick. *And soon, they're all going to realize that Dustin, their Speaker and tribemate, is gone. What will they do when they realize that it's because of me?*

# CHAPTER 3

Ellagard felt her heart pound against her ribs. Dismay and fear gripped her so fiercely that her talons quivered.

Ellagard was back in the dreaded rogue's cave, behind the waterfall of Misty Falls. Ellagard felt sick at the sight of it. It was exactly how she remembered it, all of those nights ago, when Jarquanzila had taken her there. *No!* she thought, horrified. *Not here! Not again!* Ellagard took a couple of steps backward. Then, she felt her plumage collide with something behind her. Ellagard whirled around, quickly extending her talons. She gasped, then let out a dangerous screech.

Khan, the sworn enemy of her tribe, was standing right in front of her. His eerie, dark amber gaze glittered in malice.

Ellagard swiftly lifted a talon into the air. "You'll never threaten my tribe again! You're a monster!" she screamed as she thrusted the talon forward with startling speed. It collided with Khan.

Ellagard blinked. The moment her talons touched his dark plumage, he disappeared into a cloud of black smoke. Ellagard froze, feeling her feathers rise.

Suddenly, a terrible laugh slithered through her ears. The cave began to fade away, leaving her in a void of darkness.

Ellagard drew in a shaky gasp as awful memories began to flash through her head. She crumpled slightly, burying her head in her wings.

Ellagard remembered being stuck in the empty void of Jajarii, helpless, while her tribe was being ravaged by Khan and his rogues.

She remembered Thargus, her father, and his final words, declaring her as the tribe's unexpected new leader.

She remembered the look of terror in Zander's green eyes before... before... Ellagard slammed her eyes shut, unable to allow the memory to play out in her head.

Khan's laugh sounded again. It taunted her. It mocked her. Ellagard couldn't stand it anymore. "Stop it!" she screamed.

The void was plunged into silence, and Ellagard felt as alone as ever. Tears dripped down from her eyes, and she pulled herself into a tight ball of feathers.

This wasn't the first time Ellagard had experienced this dream. In fact, ever since she became leader, this dream came to torment her every single night. The dream broke her, twisting her heart further and further whenever it played out in her head.

The dream constantly reminded her of how she had failed at her sworn duty: to protect the tribe.

In the days that had passed since Khan had raided her camp, Ellagard felt as destroyed and lost as ever. It was one thing to have an innocent dream of being the tribe's glorious leader. It was another thing to actually be it. The grief that the tribe experienced rested squarely on her shoulders. Every loss, every tear, every heartache that her tribemates felt was what she felt as well.

She *had* to feel their pain. It was her tribe now, after all. How could she not? A good leader should be one with her tribe, not above it.

Another sob gripped her, and Ellagard wrapped her wings more tightly around herself.

She had the responsibility of every single bird in the tribe in her talons. She was their leader now. And yet here she was, crying like a hatchling.

Ellagard shook her head and quickly wiped away her tears with a wing. It took a few moments, but after she collected herself, she rose to her talons. Ellagard looked around. *I know that I'll wake up soon, like I always do around now. But maybe...* she let the thought waver. *Maybe I can discover something about this dream, and why I keep having it every single night.*

Ellagard hesitated for a moment, looking out at the seemingly endless blackness of her dream. Then, without really knowing where she was going, began to walk.

Hours seemed to pass. Or were they only minutes? Perhaps it had only been a few seconds. Ellagard wasn't sure. *How far does this dream go?* she thought, frustration beginning to course through her feathers. She felt as though she had been walking for a lifetime.

Without warning, the faintest noise sounded off in the distance. "Help..." a small voice whispered.

Ellagard froze, each of her feathers beginning to bristle. Silence hung in the air. Ellagard extended her talons, then strained her ears, listening carefully.

"Help..." the voice repeated after a few seconds, this time with a note of desperation.

Ellagard looked around, her gaze sweeping the dark dream. There was not a single bird in sight. *Could it be one of my tribemates in trouble?*

she wondered, starting to feel worried. This was the first time she had dreamed this.

Usually, she would have woken up at around this point, never making it this far into the dream. What was happening? Who needed her help, and why?

Ellagard peered harder into the darkness, determined to help whoever was calling out for her.

There!

She had almost missed them. They were out there, so far away from where she stood. From this distance, they looked more like an ant than an actual peacock, if they were even a peacock at all. "Please don't worry, I'm coming!" Ellagard called out to them. *If I don't wake up by the time I get to you,* she realized darkly.

Time was running out. Ellagard could already feel herself starting to stir in the waking world. She would need to move fast. Ellagard quickly unfolded her wings, ready to fly toward the small speck in the distance. Ellagard blinked, and then let out a gasp.

The bird was gone! Ellagard couldn't believe her eyes. How could the bird disappear in less than a second? A chill ran down her spine, and she slowly extended her talons.

Suddenly, she felt something slam into her shoulder. Ellagard let out a yelp of surprise, then whirled around. Zander stood in front of her, his stunning green eyes wide with horror, and turquoise feathers bristling.

"Zander?" Ellagard breathed, feeling shock grip her. "I don't understand. How are you-"

"You have to save me, please!" he hurriedly began. "I survived, Ellagard. They're keeping me here. I-I don't know how I got to you, and I don't think that I can do it again. Look for me. Save me!"

A terrible screech abruptly tore through the dream, and the ground began to violently shake. Zander's eyes grew wide with dread.

Ellagard felt her heart pound. "Where are you?" she demanded, terrified to know that Zander had been alive this whole time, and she had done nothing to help him.

Zander opened his beak to speak. Suddenly, he was knocked to the floor as if struck by an invisible talon. His green eyes grew wide with dread. "Misty Falls!" he gasped. "Come! Please!"

Ellagard froze. Khan suddenly appeared from the shadows. He prowled forward like a tiger, amber eyes glittering. Ellagard, hiding her fear, forced herself to stand tall and to meet her brother's gaze.

*I'm not dreaming this,* she realized, panic-stricken. *It's him. This is really him. Khan is really here!*

Since Khan had previously been a Speaker, he had a special connection to Jarquanzila, and to all the other Speakers, past and present. *And that includes me,* Ellagard realized faintly.

"Hello, sister," Khan softly growled. Without warning, he leapt at Zander with his talons dangerously extended.

"No!" Ellagard screamed. As fast as she could, Ellagard darted forward to intercept Khan's blow.

But Khan was faster.

He struck down on Zander with ferocious strength. The moment Khan's talons met with the young peacock's turquoise feathers, he disappeared into a cloud of black smoke.

Ellagard let out a cry of dread, watching as she lost Zander for a second time. A grin slid over Khan's face. "You'll never save him," he teased in a slow, menacing voice.

The ground once again began to violently rumble. Khan looked around before letting out a laugh. "Farewell, Ellagard!" he spat.

Ellagard leapt at him. Just before she could land a blow, Khan disappeared within a blink of an eye.

Her dream continued to shake, fiercer and fiercer, until the movement was so strong that Ellagard couldn't even balance herself to stand. She gasped, fear flooding through her.

Without warning, the world stilled. Ellagard drew in a shaky breath, feeling her heart race. She opened her eyes and looked around, finding herself in the Peacock Tribe's camp. Ellagard was back in the waking world.

Ellagard took a long moment to collect herself before turning her gaze to the pale, morning sky above. *Zander is out there somewhere,* she told herself. Ellagard dug her talons deep into the earth, clenching her beak. *I'll bring you home, Zander,* she silently vowed. *I promise.*

# CHAPTER 4

The sound of crashing waves grew louder and louder as Cornelius flew toward the Blue Jay Tribe. His eyes watered as harsh wind whipped past his feathers. Grey storm clouds swarmed in the sky above, snuffing out the sun's warm light. The forest around Cornelius looked murky and gloomy, perfectly reflecting his mood.

All he could think about was Dustin, who was trapped and helpless inside of the nothingness of Jajarii. A darker thought suddenly gripped him. *What if he isn't even there anymore?* Cornelius couldn't help but wonder. *What if Dustin is gone for good?*

Cornelius had to force back a small whimper. Guilt struck him whenever he looked at any of the surrounding blue jays, or at Shadow. *What kind of SkyTalon am I? I've ruined everything—for everyone,* he thought, dropping his gaze to the thick canopy of trees below.

The SkyTalons and blue jay patrol had been flying for several minutes now, flying deeper and deeper into the forest. Cornelius looked around blearily. *Where is their camp?* he asked himself. There were no signs of a tribe anywhere. Had this been a trap?

Cornelius turned his attention to Shadow, who flew confidently beside him. Her gaze was clear and her head was held high. She wasn't worried. *So I won't be, either,* Cornelius told himself.

Suddenly, Myra half-folded her wings and began to dive. The rest of the patrol, and Shadow, quickly copied. Cornelius hesitated for a moment, watching as Myra and a few other blue jays disappeared into the leaves below, as if the forest itself had swallowed them up.

*This is it,* Cornelius told himself as he began to dive. *We're about the meet the Blue Jay Tribe at last, and they're all going to discover that I'm responsible for Dustin vanishing. That I'm the one responsible for losing him forever.*

Wind lashed at his face as he neared the trees below. A sudden feeling of terror curled its frozen talons around his heart, and this time his distress wasn't about Dustin. *The last time I encountered a tribe, their leader tried to destroy me and Shadow forever,* Cornelius remembered weakly. *Malik hated me the moment he saw me. He hated me so much that he sent Aquila and a few of his best Protectors to hunt us down. And it's my fault that they're gone now.*

Cornelius still felt terrible whenever he thought about the ravens. He remembered the look of terror in their eyes before the avalanche had fallen on them. Deep down Cornelius knew that if he hadn't only been worrying about saving himself, the ravens would still be here. Just like how Dustin would still be here, if only he had tried harder.

Cornelius flinched. Leaves slapped against his face as he plunged into the forest, snapping him out of his thoughts about the ravens. Within moments, Cornelius emerged on the other side, finding himself in the very heart of the Blue Jay Tribe.

The tribe's camp was completely hidden to the outside world. The forest's tree tops created a thick, dome-like roof that sheltered the tribe from the unforgiving wind outside.

Waves crashed and hissed nosily. Cornelius blinked in surprise. Up ahead, at the very back of the camp, rested a magnificent lake that stretched as far as the eye could see.

In the center of the lake, not too far from where the camp was, stood a small island. For the most part, the island was empty, hosting only a few shaken and bare shrubs. But in the center of it all was a huge, grey tree. It towered high in the sky, standing magnificently.

Cornelius felt the tree's power, just by looking at it. He knew right away that this was the Blue Jay Tribe's Life Tree.

Without warning, Myra let out an ear-splitting screech, announcing their presence to the tribe. Cornelius peeled his gaze away from the Life Tree and back to the tribe.

He let out a gasp.

Down below were countless blue jays. They were all gathered on the forest floor, huddled around a single grey boulder that rested in the center of the camp. Cornelius felt a twinge of nervousness when he realized that all eyes were glued to Shadow and him.

Panic began to ravage through Cornelius. *What if they're just like the Raven Tribe?* he wondered nervously. *I bet they all despise me already, just by knowing that I'm a tribeless pigeon.* Cornelius' breath began to come in sharp wheezes.

Myra turned her head to look back at Shadow and Cornelius. "Follow me," she ordered before gliding down to land beside the grey boulder in the center of the camp.

Cornelius reluctantly followed, feeling faint. Memories flashed through his head. He remembered the terrifyingly powerful gust of wind that had sent him plummeting from the height of the mountains to the ground below.

He remembered Malik, the Raven Tribe's leader, who had stood on a boulder just like the one Cornelius was flying toward. He flinched as he remembered the hate glowing in the raven's dark and hooded eyes.

Cornelius remembered Aquila and the other ravens. He remembered the avalanche that had swallowed them up, and the fear he felt as he watched it tumble down from the mountainside.

Cornelius felt dizzy. Cornelius felt horrified. The tribe around him began to darken as little black stars swirled around his vision. There were just too many memories, too many emotions, flooding back to him at once. *All of that pain and loss never would have happened if I hadn't interfered with the Raven Tribe,* Cornelius thought, feeling sick. *By coming here, will I end up causing just as much pain in the Blue Jay Tribe? I've already failed Dustin. Who else will I fail?*

Suddenly, something softly touched Cornelius' wingtip. He blinked, turning his head. Shadow's wingtip gently brushed against his. She gave him the smallest nod, her eyes soft with understanding. *You aren't alone,* she wordlessly told him as they neared the ground.

Cornelius drew in a shaky breath, calming himself. Together, Shadow and Cornelius landed a respectful distance in front of the boulder, a throne reserved only for the tribe's leader. Blue jays stared at the two SkyTalons in awe, their eyes as round as the full moon. But not all of them stared in excitement. Cornelius froze, shame washing over him as he listened to their hushed voices.

"Why is there a pigeon here?" one of them whispered.

"Are these the *real* SkyTalons?" another gawked.

"A pigeon? What a joke."

Cornelius forced himself to ignore them. He scanned the camp, feeling fear coil around him. Being insulted was the least of his worries right now. A dark thought crept through his head. *Somewhere in this camp could be the Shadow Within,* Cornelius realized, his heart pounding. *The bird that attacked us in Jajarii. The bird that took Dustin.*

Without warning, the whole tribe began to bow. To his surprise, even Shadow dipped her head in respect. Cornelius looked around in confusion, then let out a gasp.

Flying high over the camp was a blue jay. He circled overhead, scanning the camp below with his piercing, icy blue eyes.

Cornelius flinched as the blue jay's cold gaze raked over him. Was it Cornelius' imagination, or did the blue jay's eyes suddenly fill with anger and disgust?

Cornelius couldn't be sure, because the leader abruptly dove, landing on top of his boulder with a powerful thump that echoed through the camp. Cornelius quickly dipped his head, like Shadow was doing. *I need to follow her every move,* he told himself. *She knows the tribe's customs and traditions, and how to stay alive.*

Cornelius didn't dare to breathe, knowing that the noisy sound would bring the unwanted attention of every bird in the tribe. Cornelius could sense the leader's frosty gaze latching onto his feathers. Fear surged through him.

*Click... Click... Click...*

The leader's talons made the slightest noise with every step he took. A lifetime seemed to pass before the leader finally spoke.

"So... you two must be the SkyTalons," he mused, his slow voice like dripping icicles.

Shadow lifted her head. Just as she was about to speak, a bloodcurdling shriek tore through the silent camp. All heads lifted and turned toward the direction of the noise.

Cornelius let out a gasp.

A blue jay was flying from the Life Tree island, panic glistening in her eyes. She flew lopsidedly, her wings flapping desperately to maintain her balance. The birdess was carrying something in her talons. Cornelius squinted, unsure of what it could be from this distance.

The birdess swooped into the center of the camp, landing in between the tribe's leader and the two SkyTalons. She gently placed down whatever she had been carrying, then took a few steps backward.

The leader's eyes grew wide with horror. Gasps and fearful murmurs swarmed through the camp. Cornelius felt sick, swaying slightly.

All eyes were on the limp, small shape of Dustin.

# CHAPTER 5

The leader of the Blue Jay Tribe let out a gasp of horror, eyes wide with concern. He hurriedly threw open his wings and swooped down toward Dustin. Cornelius took a few steps backward, his head spinning with disbelief. *Dustin? How is this possible?* he wondered. *How is he still here?*

Countless fearful voices erupted throughout the camp. The surrounding blue jays exchanged worried looks, no bird certain of what they should do next. Had this been an attack? Or an accident? Should they raise their defenses, or should they prepare for an all-out war?

Cornelius' gaze was stuck on Dustin and the leader. He watched, feeling sick, as the leader hurriedly snapped for a Healer to come. Panic glistened in the leader's eyes, his pale-blue feathers beginning to flare.

It unnerved Cornelius to see the leader's demeanour change so abruptly. Suddenly, a thought struck Cornelius, making him flinch. *He isn't just worried about his tribemate's safety,* Cornelius realized, watching as the leader began to pace back and forth. *He's worried about his hatchling!*

Suddenly, the leader's head shot up. With a clenched beak, he looked at Cornelius with eyes like two frozen chips of ice. Cornelius recoiled, feeling fear pour over him. *He knows,* he realized with a jolt. *He knows that this is my fault!*

The air around Cornelius began to feel thinner and thinner. The leader started to slowly prowl toward him and Shadow, malice making his gaze hard. Fear froze Cornelius to the spot. The leader was a feather's length in front of him when he lifted a pointed, thorn-sharp talon into the air.

"Cornelius!" Shadow cried, immediately springing forward to defend her fellow SkyTalon.

Cornelius gasped, slamming his eyes shut. To his surprise, he found himself being pulled forward, almost stumbling to the ground from the force of it. Cornelius blinked, opening his eyes, and found himself face-to-face with the leader.

The blue jay's frosty eyes reflected the storm clouds outside of the camp as they bore into Cornelius. A long, long moment passed before the leader spoke. "If you're anything like *him*, I know that you can save Dustin," he growled at Cornelius.

Slowly, the leader released his sharp grip on Cornelius' shoulder and took a step back. "Save my son, SkyTalons... please," he said.

Cornelius and Shadow exchanged a nervous look. *If I'm anything like him?* Cornelius wondered, bewildered. He thought about this for a moment, unsure of who the leader was referring to. But that moment didn't last long. Shadow began to walk forward, signaling for Cornelius to do the same.

By now, a talonful of Healers had gathered around Dustin, each frantically debating with one another. No bird seemed certain on what should be done. As the two SkyTalons approached, one of the Healers broke away from the crowd, putting herself between them and Dustin. She let out a warning cry. "Please, don't come any closer," she cautioned.

"Let them through, Elizabeth," the leader ordered, watching her and the SkyTalons carefully. Elizabeth looked puzzled for a moment, then her demeanour shifted into one of defiance. "But Atticus, these are strangers! How do we know that we can trust them, especially with your son?" she questioned.

Atticus' glare was all Elizabeth needed for an answer. With a final untrusting look at Shadow and Cornelius, she reluctantly stepped aside, motioning for her fellow Healers to do the same.

The tribe suddenly fell silent as they watched the two SkyTalons approach Dustin.

Cornelius felt a pang of unease. *What are we supposed to do?* he asked himself. *I have no idea how we can help Dustin. Just because we're SkyTalons, they expect us to have all the answers. But... we just don't.*

Cornelius glanced at Shadow, and from the uncertainty in her eyes, she seemed to be thinking the exact same thing. A few silent moments passed. Guilt flooded through him as he silently stared down at the unmoving shape of Dustin. He looked so small... so helpless. And it was all Cornelius' fault.

*I'm so sorry!* he thought.

Suddenly, an icy chill crept along Cornelius' feathers. He stiffened, surprised. Cornelius remembered feeling something like this, all the way back in the city, before he had learned of his destiny to be a SkyTalon.

Cornelius had felt this chill, just before he had met with Jarquanzila for the first time.

*Could it really be him?* he wondered. The roar of the lake just a couple of wing lengths away from him abruptly silenced into nothingness. The only sound that could be heard was Cornelius' and

Shadow's breathing. Shadow shot Cornelius a questioning look, her eyes seeming to ask *is this happening to you, too?* Cornelius slowly nodded.

"I will bring Dustin back to you," came Jarquanzila's voice. "But it won't be without consequences."

Cornelius blinked. He looked around at the tribe. No bird seemed aware of Jarquanzila's presence. Atticus abruptly turned away, looking worried. Cornelius watched him warily.

"From now on, you two will stand alone," Jarquanzila finished. Without warning, the roar of the lake and the howl of the wind outside the camp all returned at once. The sudden noise struck Cornelius like talons, making him flinch.

Dustin abruptly stirred, letting out a gasp as he caught his breath. His blue eyes slowly opened, and they instantly filled with surprise. The tribe was staring at him, shocked. Every bird was too stunned to even move. Dustin shrunk slightly, looking embarrassed. "What... what happened?" he asked groggily.

Just before Cornelius could answer, Atticus barged his way forward. He pushed past Shadow and Cornelius, quickly hurrying to reach his son. To Cornelius' surprise, Dustin's gaze suddenly turned cold; almost frostier than Atticus'. His beak clenched, and his feathers bristled. A tense moment passed before Dustin rose to his talons, swaying slightly as he stood in between Shadow and Cornelius. He turned his gaze toward the tribe.

"It's time you all learnt the truth about me," Dustin began, speaking as loud as he could manage. The silent tribe watched Dustin in anticipation. The small blue jay hesitated for a moment, looking worried, before speaking again. "I am the third SkyTalon."

The tribe stared in awe. Without warning, thunder boomed, the powerful noise reverberating through the forest.

A blue light suddenly erupted in the distance, flooding the camp. All heads turned toward the Life Tree in the distance. The stone-like tree was aglow, cutting through the darkness of the storm, and outlining every one of the SkyTalon's feathers with its light.

Cornelius froze, feeling a sudden surge of power flow through his veins. He felt as though he could fly through any storm, fight any darkness that threatened the tribes, and help any bird who needed him. It was like a piece of Cornelius, one that he had never known was missing, had finally returned to him. He turned to look at his fellow SkyTalons, and he could tell that they felt the same way.

Gasps exploded around the tribe.

"It's them! It's really the SkyTalons!"

"We're saved!"

"Things will finally be okay now!"

Cornelius felt unstoppable as their praise filled the air. But the feeling was abruptly cut short. Darkness slammed into Cornelius, making him gasp. All that feeling of power and certainty was snuffed out in a matter of seconds. Cornelius recoiled, feeling icy fear pulse through him. *The Shadow Within must be doing this,* he realized with a jolt. Cornelius wildly scanned the many cheering faces of the Blue Jay Tribe, desperate to find the source of this dark energy.

His gaze suddenly halted on Atticus.

The tribe's leader stood motionlessly amongst the crowd. His head was lowered and his feathers were rigid. Darkness fell over him, his plumage murky with shadows, while the SkyTalons were showered in light. Atticus' icy eyes were hooded as he stared at Shadow. His gaze then slithered over to Dustin. Then, finally, his empty stare latched onto Cornelius. A terrible anger burned in his eyes.

Cornelius felt another wave of darkness collide into him, almost making him stagger backward.

"SkyTalons! SkyTalons! SkyTalons!" the tribe cheered in unison, distracting Cornelius. For the briefest of moments, Cornelius turned his attention away from Atticus. And when he went to return it, the tribe's leader was nowhere to be seen.

# Chapter 6

Ellagard felt the ground sway from under her talons. She drew in a deep breath to steady her nerves. Countless thoughts raced through her head.

*Zander is alive?* Ellagard thought. *But how? I thought I watched him...* Ellagard shook her head, as if doing so would clear the memory. It was too painful to relive.

*He's been out there this whole time, and yet I did nothing to help him.* Guilt began to gnaw at her heart. She had so many questions, and very few answers.

The sun was beginning to rise, outlining the peacefully silent jungle in a yellow glow. A soft breeze swooshed through her plumage and the trees overhead, making their leaves rustle. Ellagard, as usual, was the first to awake. She often found herself sleeping less and less these nights, and when she did, her slumber was disturbed by awful nightmares.

Ellagard rose to her talons, and began to pace back and forth under the branches of the Life Tree. Ellagard froze as a thought suddenly struck her.

How could she have forgotten?

She had to see to her trainees, Alexia and Cassidy, today for battle practice. Ellagard let out a groan of annoyance, burying her head deep into her wings. For a moment, she had almost forgotten about them. She blinked, feeling shame wash over her feathers. *How could I have forgotten about my own trainees?* Ellagard wondered, releasing a heavy sigh. And on top of them, she had a whole tribe to run *and* she had to uncover the secrets of Zander's mysterious appearance.

Ellagard blinked, determination rushing through her veins. *I'll go and find Zander right now, before the tribe wakes up!* she boldly thought. Zander needed Ellagard's help, and he wouldn't have to wait a second longer to get it!

Just as Ellagard was about to start her quest and walk out of the camp, the realization of being the tribe's leader hit her. Ellagard clenched her beak in frustration, casting a longing look to the territory outside of the camp. She hated all of the boring responsibilities (like settling disputes between two disagreeing tribemates) that tethered her to the tribe, now that she was leader. Oh, how her talons itched to be out there *doing something.*

Ellagard reluctantly headed back under the branches of the Life Tree and sat down. Frustration pulsed through her.

*I'm not the commander of the Protectors anymore, that's Cyprus' job,* she reminded herself, distractedly digging her talons in and out of the dirt. *I'm the leader of the entire tribe now. I can't take risks like I used to. I need to think about this logically. We can't afford to send a whole patrol to Misty Falls, that would leave the camp vulnerable. And that would also risk too many Protectors for just one peacock.*

Ellagard frowned, running all of her options through her head. Nothing seemed to workall except for one thought that kept on nagging at her. *But what if I do just go alone?* she wondered. *Could I sneak in and rescue Zander unnoticed? But then what if I'm spotted, and something terrible happens? The tribe would be leaderless, as I don't have a second-in-command yet,* she thought darkly.

That was another problem weighing her down. A few days after she had lost Thargus, her adoptive father and previous leader of the tribe, Ellagard had approached Cyprus.

Even though they had always been rivals, fighting for their father's attention and position as leader, Ellagard still found a twinge of respect for him. She had offered the position as second-in-command to Cyprus, but he had only lashed out and refused to speak with her.

Cyprus wasn't the same after Khan's attack. He barely spoke to anyone, or left the shelter of the sleeping-dens. On the few times that Cyprus did, he silently trudged through the camp like a ghost, keeping his head low and eyes planted firmly to the ground.

Now, Ellagard felt a flash of pity for him, feeling as though her feathers were made out of stone. *It must be hard for him,* she grimly thought, watching as her tribemates began to stir. The first patrol of the day left the camp. *Thargus was the only bird that Cyprus thought cared about him. And the last thing Thargus did was take away his leadership, right in front of him.*

Ellagard sighed. *No wonder he doesn't want to speak with me.* Lost in her thoughts of guilt and regret, Ellagard hadn't noticed Alexia as she slowly crept up behind her. The small peacock's eyes flashed playfully. "Surprise!" she called as she pounced on her teacher.

Ellagard, forcing on a smile, pretended to be wounded. "Oh no, the fiercest rogue in the jungle has finally gotten me!" she dramatically gasped before heavily sinking to the floor. "The horror! The pain!"

Alexia giggled. "Well, I did have one of the best Protectors, like, in the history of ever, to teach me," she teased, helping Ellagard up. They both laughed.

*Her stealth is coming along nicely,* Ellagard thought in satisfaction, starting to feel slightly better. She was glad to have a friend like Alexia with her during these difficult times. When things got tough for one of them, the other would be there to support them.

Ellagard paused, watching as Alexia's sister, Cassidy, slowly trudged forward. Her gaze was blank, and her movements looked heavy. Ellagard frowned, feeling a pang of guilt for her trainee. *Cassidy and Alexia had lost their brother during Khan's invasion,* she remembered. *They had both struggled with their grief for a while. Alexia seems as though she's finally beginning to recover. But Cassidy...*

Ellagard let out a sigh.

Suddenly, frustration burned through her. *Maybe if Jarquanzila didn't keep me stuck in that terrible void, their brother would still be here,* she thought. *I could have helped the whole tribe. We could have even won that battle, and have finally driven the rogues away for good!*

Ellagard felt the urge to score her talons through the dirt. She closed her eyes for a moment and drew in a deep breath. *Being in a fit of rage won't change anything,* she told herself. *Now that I'm leader, I'll need to control my temper more than ever before.*

Ellagard walked over to Cassidy and gently placed her wing on her shoulder. "I'd understand if you want to take today off," she said.

To her surprise, Cassidy stiffened, her eyes beginning to blaze with rage. "No!" she shouted. "I need to train, and I need to get stronger. It's my fault that he's gone now. If I had only been more experienced... more brave... then he would still be here. I can't let anything happen like that again. *Never* again," she finished while looking at Alexia.

Ellagard felt a flash of surprise. That was exactly how she had felt after she had lost her own brother, Felix, to an ocelot attack seemingly lifetimes ago. She remembered with a slash of guilt how she had to choose between Khan—who had been a helpless, weak Speaker at the time—and Felix. They both had been fighting with ocelots.

Khan had been backed against the stone-like wall of the Life Tree, desperately lashing out at the creature with feeble swipes. Felix had been such a promising Protector. Ellagard never would have thought that by rushing to Khan's aid, she would have been responsible for Felix's destruction.

To this day, Ellagard still found herself regretting her choice. If only she had just stayed with her brother, Khan never would have begun his rebellion, Thargus would still be leader, and life would be better for everyone. Ellagard forced herself to break away from her painful memories. She couldn't change the past.

Ellagard offered Cassidy a small nod. "I understand how you feel," she murmured. Standing up straighter, she turned toward the jungle outside of the camp. "Let's go."

As she walked, with Cassidy and Alexia on her heels, Ellagard began to feel a prickle of unease. Something just wasn't sitting right with her. Ellagard warily looked around, nervousness sliding down her spine like a drop of freezing water. Everything looked fine, so then why didn't it feel like it?

Suddenly, a powerful gust of wind whipped through the trees, its chill biting at any peacock bold enough to stand in its path. Ellagard watched as a large, dead leaf tumbled past her talons as it got caught up in the wind.

The camp was plunged into a deathly silence. Not even a hatchling dared to speak. The peacocks within the camp exchanged worried glances. They could tell that something was wrong as well.

Without warning, a blood-curdling scream tore through the silence. A patrol rushed into the camp, each peacock panting to catch their breath. Leading the patrol was a beautiful, white peacock. She had splotches of black, freckle-like dots around her yellow eyes, which were wide with horror.

Murmurs of shock and concern filled the air.

Ellagard stiffened. She quickly signaled to her trainees to wait before darting forward to meet the patrol. "What has happened?" she sharply asked, feeling the feathers on her neck start to bristle. The black and white peacock trembled slightly.

"Rogues!" she cried, dread etched in her gaze. "There are rogues invading the tribe!"

# CHAPTER 7

Sunlight dappled the calm forest around Cornelius. He slowly blinked, opening his eyes, as he began to awaken. The branch he was perched on swayed slightly in the warm breeze. He let out a huge yawn and took in the scene around him.

The tribe was peaceful—a little bit too peaceful if you asked Cornelius. He watched the blue jays down below on the forest floor warily while they worked. Healers were chatting happily to one another as they sorted their herbs. Protectors practiced their fighting moves, laughing good-humouredly whenever one of their friends messed up. Hatchlings ran around, chasing fallen leaves as they got caught up in a breeze. Patrols came in and out of the camp. One was attended by Shadow, who was having a friendly conversation with Alessandra.

Cornelius blinked. *This is nothing like the strict, cold Raven Tribe,* he realized. *Birds here actually seem... happy.*

It had been a couple of days since Cornelius and Shadow had arrived at the Blue Jay Tribe. At first, Cornelius had been terrified, unable to sleep and unable to relax. Fear had coiled around him like a vicious snake, refusing to let go.

Jarquanzila's ominous warning of a terrible threat—of the Shadow Within—was constantly on the back of his mind. Cornelius was convinced that Atticus was hiding something. He just knew, deep in his heart, that the leader was planning something horrible. But, the more Cornelius watched the leader in secret, the less Cornelius found to worry about. Atticus acted normal. He was respectful and kind to all his tribemates. He worked hard, always doing his part to help out when he could. Cornelius had even found him joining some patrols here and there. Atticus was respected by all of the tribe. No bird seemed to fear him, not like how Malik was feared. Every bird, including Shadow, seemed to trust Atticus. Every bird except for two: Cornelius and Dustin.

Now, Cornelius drew in a deep breath. He had been planning to speak with Dustin in private ever since the young blue jay had awoken from Jajarii. Not only to thank him for saving his life, but to ask him a very risky question... could his father, Atticus, be the Shadow Within?

Cornelius sighed. He didn't know how Dustin would react to this question. If Cornelius asked him, would Dustin end up telling his father about Cornelius' suspicions? Or would Dustin agree with Cornelius? *Dustin has been in the Blue Jay Tribe for far longer than Shadow and I have,* Cornelius thought, scanning the tribe below for the young bird. *If any bird would have an idea of who the Shadow Within could be, that bird would be Dustin.*

Cornelius spotted him after a few seconds of searching. Dustin sat amongst the Healers in their section of the camp, as he normally did these days. Ever since Dustin had awakened from Jajarii, he had been confined to the camp, always having a Healer close by to watch him. Atticus had been the one to order this, much to Elizabeth's approval. They both wanted to make sure that Dustin was in perfect condition before letting him out of their sights.

Cornelius unfolded his wings and swooped down to the forest floor below. He landed a respectful distance away from the Healers, walking the rest of the way to Dustin. The young blue jay was playing with a group of hatchlings, who bounced around him excitedly.

"Grr, I'm Khan, and I'm here to destroy you pesky SkyTalon!" one of them squealed before leaping on top of Dustin, pelting him with her tiny talons.

"Oh no, you got me!" he gasped. Dustin dramatically staggered backward, then fell to the ground. Just as he was about to rise to his talons, Dustin was immediately swarmed by the group of tiny hatchlings as they jumped onto him. Dustin fell over for real this time with a chuckle, becoming buried under their feathers. Cornelius grinned, finding Dustin's laughter contagious. But the moment didn't last long before Elizabeth rushed over, shooing the hatchlings away with her wing. "Go on," she urged. "This mighty SkyTalon needs his rest."

Dustin watched them scamper off sadly before turning his head and looking away. Elizabeth offered Dustin a small smile. "Sorry, but it's for the best," she murmured before turning around and returning to her work. Dustin sunk down into his plumage, releasing a heavy sigh. He suddenly caught sight of Cornelius lingering awkwardly a few wing lengths away. Almost immediately, Dustin put on a smile, his eyes brightening as if nothing had been wrong.

"Hi, Cornelius," Dustin cheered, walking over to him.

Cornelius smiled. "Hey, Dustin," he replied happily.

Cornelius looked over at Elizabeth, who was watching him carefully. She wouldn't dare interrupt Cornelius, a SkyTalon and guest of the tribe, despite how much she wanted to. Cornelius shifted uncomfortably as she continued to stare. Then, he returned his attention to Dustin, who was looking at him eagerly. "Do you think that we can go for a flight together? Just the two of us?" Cornelius asked. "There's some things that I want to tell you."

Dustin looked taken aback. "Uh, sure," he replied. He suddenly looked disappointed. "But I don't think that I can." He gestured at Elizabeth with his eyes before letting out a heavy sigh.

Cornelius felt a stab of annoyance. This was important! He needed answers about Atticus. If the leader truly was the Shadow Within, he had to stop him as soon as he could. *I'm not going to let Atticus destroy the tribes just because Elizabeth is being clingy to Dustin,* he told himself. Cornelius walked past Dustin, heading toward the Healer.

Elizabeth blinked at Cornelius as he came to stop a wing length in front of her. "Hello," she said politely, dipping her head as a show of respect. Cornelius quickly copied before lifting his head and standing as confidently as he could. "I've been speaking with Shadow," he lied, "and we both agree that Dustin has been resting for long enough. As SkyTalons, we need to be ready for any threats that may come our way, and we can't do that if Dustin is kept resting. We all need to be at our best, and alert at all times."

Elizabeth was silent for a long, long moment. After a few seconds she reluctantly nodded. "Of course," she sighed. "I understand." Cornelius felt a flash of satisfaction. Just as he was about to open his beak to speak, Dustin rushed forward, his eyes glittering with joy. "Thank you, aunt Elizabeth!" he cried, wrapping his wings around her.

Cornelius recoiled. *Aunt Elizabeth?* His mind echoed. *Oh no. But if she's Dustin's aunt, then that means that Atticus and her are family!*

*That explains why they always seem so close, and are always agreeing with one another.* A dark, terrifying thought suddenly struck him. *If Atticus really is the Shadow Within, then that means that Elizabeth is probably working with him.*

Elizabeth wrapped her wings around Dustin, looking at him fondly. Then, her gaze flickered over to Cornelius. "You be careful out there," she said slowly, almost threateningly. "And keep Dustin safe."

Cornelius suddenly felt his throat turn dry. He nodded vigorously, forcing himself to meet her piercing gaze. After a few long seconds, Elizabeth broke away from Dustin's hug. She smiled at him lovingly. Then, she turned around and flew off, leaving Cornelius feeling horrified.


The sky was bright and blue, not a single cloud in sight. The sun was a happy colour of yellow as it spread its warmth all across the forest. Up ahead, very far in the distance, proudly stood the mountains that Shadow and Cornelius had crossed not too long ago.

Dustin drew in a deep breath, relishing the fresh, crisp breeze. Then he did a loop in the air for fun. He looked at Cornelius happily. "I can't tell you how amazing it is to be able to stretch my wings again!" he exclaimed. Cornelius forced himself to smile at him. Dustin continued on, buzzing with excitement. "I thought that I would never be able to leave the camp again," he said, only half-joking. "You're the best, thank you, Cornelius!"

*He seems so happy,* Cornelius thought. He suddenly remembered the frosty look that Dustin had thrown at Atticus a couple of days ago.

*Something clearly happened between them, and I can only wonder what. Would it be wrong to sour Dustin's mood by mentioning his father now?* he wondered.

Cornelius paused for a moment, thinking carefully. But that moment didn't last long. Dustin turned to look at him expectantly. "So, what did you want to ask me?" he asked invitingly. Cornelius flinched. *I can't avoid bringing it up now,* he realized. *And it might be for the best this way.* Cornelius hesitated before opening his beak to speak. Just before the words could come out, a patch of trees below began to violently shake.

Suddenly, a huge, white shape burst out of the forest. It rose up to meet the two SkyTalons, letting out a furious screech. Cornelius barely had enough time to avoid the bird. He quickly darted to the side, just missing getting slapped by its massive wing.

Cornelius gasped, shrinking backward. His eyes grew wide with dread. *It's a seagull!* he realized, terrified. Back in his home in the city, seagulls had ruled many parts of the land. If any pigeon had dared to enter into their territory, well... that pigeon was never seen again. The seagulls were mean, fierce, and at one point had almost driven away Cornelius' flock for good. *For the longest time, the seagulls had ruled the city. Not us pigeons,* he remembered darkly. *My flock had almost lost everything to them. I had almost lost everything to them. I had almost...* he quickly pushed away the memory, refusing to let it play out in his head. He instinctively looked down at his side for a moment before turning his gaze back to the seagull.

The seagull had fixed its beady, yellow eye onto Cornelius. She stared at him for a long, long moment. Then, the seagull turned her gaze onto Dustin. Her eyes suddenly blazed with anger. "You've passed the border," she hissed in a slow, dangerous voice. "Leave now, while I still allow it."

Cornelius eyed the seagull warily, noticing how huge she was compared to Dustin and himself. A thought suddenly struck Cornelius. *Are these the birds that have been threatening the tribe?* he wondered, starting to feel worried. *Seagulls aren't birds to be taken lightly, I've experienced that first-taloned.*

Instinctively, Cornelius began to extend his talons, ready to defend Dustin, no matter what the cost was. The seagull's gaze travelled down to Cornelius' talons. She immediately noticed Cornelius' sudden rise in defensiveness. "Save your energy," she told Cornelius slowly, locking eyes with him. "This will all be settled soon enough, and you'll get your fair share of battle."

Dustin glared at the seagull, his beak clenching. He nudged Cornelius forward, shooting the seagull a final bitter look before leading the way back toward the tribe. Cornelius slowly followed Dustin, his head beginning to spin with unanswered questions. The seagull watched them go before diving back down into the cover of the forest.

Cornelius felt sick as the seagull's words echoed through his head. *"This will all be settled soon enough, and you'll get your fair share of battle."*

# CHAPTER 8

A full moon hung in the inky night sky, outlining the forest below in a silver glow. Countless glittering stars danced in the blackness, their light reflected in the lake as its smooth waves lapped gently against the pebble-filled shore. It was the night of the Speaker's meeting.

Countless blue jays were perched all around Cornelius as he restlessly slept. Their soft snores filled the still night. But despite how calm the forest was, Cornelius felt nothing but fear surging through his veins. Dark, terrible dreams slithered through Cornelius' head, making him whimper slightly.

Right now, Cornelius was dreaming about the Blue Jay Tribe. The camp was deserted, not a single bird in sight. The night was dark and foggy, the moon's light snuffed out from the thick clouds swirling overhead. Cornelius could barely see where he was putting his own talons. "Hello?" he warily called out, not yet aware that this was just a nightmare. "Shadow? Dustin? Are you here?"

Suddenly, he spotted them far in the distance. Their backs were turned to Cornelius, and they talked in hushed voices. Relief flooded through him. Cornelius unfolded his wings, ready to fly toward his friends. Just before he could take off, Shadow and Dustin shot into the air, leaving Cornelius all alone. Their mocking laughter faded into the night. "No, wait!" he called out to them as they disappeared into the thick fog. "Where are you going? Please come back!"

"They won't come back, Cornelius," a voice said, almost jeeringly. "No bird will. You're all alone."

Cornelius shook his head, forcing his fear down. "That isn't true," he murmured. "I trust Shadow completely. If she left, then it's for a very good reason. I know that she'll be back as soon as she can. And so will Dustin. We're a team..."

The voice let out a scornful laugh. "You're no team," it huffed. "How can you be a team when they *abandoned* you here? That doesn't sound very team-like to me, now does it?"

Cornelius looked around at the still, eerie forest, feeling his heart begin to sink. *It's true, they did leave me here,* Cornelius realized, feeling the sting of betrayal slash its cruel talons across his heart. *Why would they do this to me?* Cornelius wondered. He thought about this for a long time, feeling more and more puzzled by the second. *But it doesn't make sense. Why* would *they leave me here? They would never have abandoned me; they aren't those kind of birds. And if they were going somewhere, then they would have just said so.*

The sudden realization struck him.

This wasn't real, none of it was!

Cornelius would never dream up something like this. So then, who... or what... was? Cornelius drew in a sharp gasp. "Who are you?" he demanded. "And what do you want?"

The mysterious voice chuckled. "We've met already, briefly," it said teasingly. "And I'm here because I have a proposition for you."

Cornelius blinked, and when he opened his eyes again, he let out a gasp of surprise. Fear thundered through his plumage, making his talons tremble. Cornelius found himself face-to-face with the bird who had attacked the SkyTalons in Jajarii. The bird who had almost taken Dustin forever. The bird who was known as the Shadow Within.

"Hello, Cornelius," they said.

Cornelius took a step backward, extending his trembling talons. "Why are you doing this?" was the first thing that managed to escape his beak. "Why do you want to hurt the tribes? To hurt us?"

The Shadow Within smiled, the gesture causing the blobs of darkness masking their plumage to shift slightly. "I want to hurt the tribes because I hate everything about them," they bluntly replied. "And I don't want to hurt you, Cornelius. I want you to join me. Join us."

Cornelius gulped. "Us?" he repeated weakly. "There's more of you?" *I was right,* Cornelius realized. *Atticus and Elizabeth are working together. This bird must be one of them. But I can't let them know that I've figured out who they are. That could end... badly. I'll play this out for as long as I can.*

The Shadow Within nodded. "Yes. Us," they stated.

"But why would I *ever* join birds who attacked Dustin and Shadow, my friends, back in Jajarii?" he demanded. "Why would I ever join birds who tried to end all three of us?"

The shadow stared at Cornelius unblinkingly for a few heartbeats. "Because you're just like us," they said at last. "You want justice. You want a better world. You want peace. And, most importantly, you want to stop those who get in the way of that. We aren't as different as you think, Cornelius."

Cornelius felt himself tremble. But this time it wasn't caused by fear. It was caused by rage. "We are nothing alike!" Cornelius spat. "You birds are prepared to hurt others to get what you want. I'm not, and I never will be!"

The shadow grinned. "Of course, of course," they said smoothly. "Of course you won't hurt others to get what you want. I'm sure Aquila and those other ravens would agree with you. Oh wait, they can't. Why? Because they're buried under a mountain's worth of snow and ice."

Cornelius flinched. The shadow continued on, their black eyes narrowed. "The talk of the tribes these days is that after you're all done getting rid of us, the Shadows Within, you're going to move on to the Peacock Tribe. To sort out Khan, right?" they asked. The more they spoke, the more anger slipped into their voice. "How do you plan on getting Khan to stop? By having a polite chat with him? By ending the biggest war of the tribes with smiles and friendship? I'm sorry, SkyTalon, but the real word just does *not* work like that!"

Cornelius suddenly felt dizzy. Fear, guilt, and confusion all came rushing down on him. The truth was, Cornelius had no idea how he was going to stop Khan. A part of him never wanted to admit the truth, while another part of him knew that there was only one way to restore peace to the tribes. And that way was through violence and pain. Cornelius closed his eyes, feeling hollow.

The bird tipped their shadow-streaked head to the side. "I see I've touched a nerve," they taunted, smirking. "But sometimes the truth needs to be learned the hard way. Come with me, Cornelius. With us.

We all want the same thing in the end. Why waste time fighting against each other to get it?"

They extended a shadowy wing, waiting for Cornelius to reach out and take it.

Cornelius blinked at them. Then, slowly, Cornelius unfolded his own wing and moved it forward toward them.

With a blaze of anger, Cornelius smacked the shadow's wing away from him. He swiftly lifted a talon and latched it onto the shadow's shoulder, digging his claws deep into their plumage. Then, he roughly pulled them closer. Cornelius stared straight into their eyes. The shadow shrunk slightly, taken aback. "I'm going to uncover the truth about you," Cornelius growled. "All of you! You aren't as smart as you think you are. Shadow, Dustin and I will save this tribe, and every other tribe, in our own way. I'll never let you hurt another bird again!"

The shadow broke away from Cornelius with a dangerous screech. "Don't be so sure!" they yelled, their shadowy feathers flaring. They took a few steps backward, into the darkness, and disappeared within a blink of an eye.

Without warning, Cornelius' dream began to violently shake. It was so fierce that he almost lost his balance. "Wake up, Cornelius!" the shadow's voice sneered. The rumbling became stronger and stronger by the second. "Wake up," they repeated. Cornelius lost his balance and began to tumble, fear surging through him.

Cornelius abruptly snapped opened his eyes, finding himself back in the real Blue Jay Tribe, in the waking world. He blinked, startled, as Shadow stood over him. She shook him with her wings, her eyes wide with panic. "Wake up!" she demanded. Screams and furious cries filled the night sky. Blue jays darted all around the camp, each hurrying from one place to the next. Cornelius felt himself freeze.

There were seagulls everywhere!

Suddenly, an ear-splitting screech exploded overhead, and a powerful gust of wind tore by. A seagull crashed into Shadow, knocking her off of the branch with a sickening thump. The two birds fought viciously as they fell toward the ground. Black and white feathers alike were torn and scattered.

Just as Cornelius was about to swoop down to defend Shadow, a seagull came rushing toward him at full speed. Fear coiled around Cornelius, and he felt his heartbeat quicken.

For just a moment, he was taken back to that horrible day in the city. Even though the memory had taken place so many years before, it was still as painful and clear as ever. He remembered the cold, sharp points of each of the seagull's talons on his shoulder. He remembered Jemma and Xavier, his siblings, and how they had been frozen with fear as they watched helplessly. They had known what was about to happen just as well as Cornelius had. He remembered–

There wasn't enough time to remember!

The seagull abruptly shot his talons forward, extending them. With only a second left to spare, Cornelius dove off of the branch and flew away as fast as he could. *I just can't face a seagull,* he thought. *I'm not brave enough!*

Without warning, cheers of victory exploded through the camp. Surprised, Cornelius whirled around and watched as the last couple of seagulls were chased out of the camp and into the forest beyond. He let out a sigh of relief. The tribe had won, and no bird looked seriously injured. Cornelius scanned the camp, taking in the destruction that the battle had caused. Branches had been broken, causing twigs and leaves to become scattered all over the forest floor.

Cornelius' gaze continued to travel until it halted on the Life Tree island in the distance. He drew in a shaky gasp. Dustin stood limply on one of the branches, his head drooping. He looked dizzy as he clutched the branch for support. But Dustin wasn't the only thing worrying Cornelius now. All around the Life Tree island were the broken, destroyed branches of the stone-like tree. A cloud of dust hung around the island, causing Dustin to cough. Cornelius rushed forward and landed at his friend's side. Dustin looked at him weakly.

"Dustin, what happened?" he hurriedly asked. "Should I get a Healer? What... what do I do?"

Dustin shook his head, looking exhausted. "Nothing," he murmured. "I'm fine... Speaker meeting... Tree destroyed while it happened... Couldn't leave Jajarii properly..."

Suddenly, a massive wave of darkness slammed into Cornelius, causing him to flinch. The air started to feel thin. Just as it was about to subside, the darkness only became stronger and stronger. It gripped Cornelius like frozen talons.

Atticus was staring at him from across the lake.

# CHAPTER 9

Cornelius felt another wave of darkness collide into him. It slithered through his plumage, biting at him with icy fangs. Atticus looked furious, his gaze darting from Cornelius to Dustin. His beak was clenched and his feathers were flared slightly.

Elizabeth suddenly swooped down and landed beside Atticus. She followed his gaze curiously, then let out a gasp when she laid eyes on the wreckage of the Life Tree. Elizabeth quickly lowered her head and whispered something into Atticus' ear. The leader slowly nodded. Elizabeth gave Dustin and the Life Tree a final distraught look before throwing a cold glare at Cornelius. Then, she unfolded her wings and flew off into the camp.

Atticus lingered for just a few moments longer. His frosty gaze was locked onto Cornelius now. He stared at him with eyes like two chips of ice. Darkness crawled through the pigeon's feathers like ants.

Then, Atticus slowly turned around and prowled off into the shadows. Cornelius let out a gasp of relief as all feelings of darkness lifted off of him.

*I was right, I have to be!* Cornelius thought. *Elizabeth and Atticus are both the Shadows Within. They're behind everything—the seagulls and their invasion, us being attacked in Jajarii, those feelings of darkness...* His head began to swim.

He remembered the shadow, who was either Atticus or Elizabeth, in his dream. They had told Cornelius that they wanted justice for something. But he could only wonder what that could be.

Dustin let out a groan, pulling Cornelius away from his thoughts. Cornelius turned to the small blue jay, starting to feel worried. "Will you be okay?" he gently asked.

Dustin's feathers suddenly started to bristle. "No!" he snapped. "I won't be okay. Look around, Cornelius! The Life Tree, the thing I swore to take care of, was damaged. Now we're a few branches closer to the whole tribe being lost forever, and it's all my fault." Angry tears dripped from his eyes, soaking his blue feathers.

The flapping of wingbeats suddenly sounded nearby. Shadow circled overhead, her dark feathers blending in with the inky night sky. She looked down at the damaged Life Tree nervously. Shadow caught sight of Cornelius and Dustin, then half-folded her wings and began to dive. The stone-like branch creaked slightly as Shadow landed on it.

By now, Dustin had buried his head into his wings, his soft sobs filling the silence.

Shadow glanced at him, frowning. Then, she gave Cornelius a questioning look. Cornelius signalled for her to follow him, then glided over to a nearby branch.

"What happened to Dustin?" Shadow asked once they were out of earshot. Cornelius sighed, feeling defeated. "He blames himself for the Life Tree being damaged," he explained sadly.

Shadow looked over her shoulder to glance at the crying blue jay. "Poor Dustin," she murmured. "He's barely older than a hatchling. The responsibility of his tribe's Life Tree is already strenuous, but blaming himself too..." she trailed off, eyes glittering with pity for her fellow SkyTalon. Without warning, she unfolded her wings and flew over to him. Cornelius blinked, then quickly hurried to follow her.

Shadow landed beside Dustin. To Cornelius' surprise, Shadow slowly lifted one of her talons. She hesitated for a moment before gently placing it on Dustin's shoulder.

Dustin's head shot up, his eyes wide and soft from crying. He gazed at the raven warily.

"I know what it's like to blame yourself," she gently began. "It's one of the worst feelings in the world. And Sometimes... sometimes that pain just doesn't go away. For most of my life I've been blaming myself for things, and I still do. But I've learned that it's best not to keep on worrying about things that you can't change, but instead focus on things that you can." As she spoke, she watched as the sun slowly rose in the distance, marking the beginning of a new day.

Dustin was silent for a long moment. "But how?" he breathed. "How can I change anything now?"

Shadow abruptly rose to her talons, then unfolded her long wings. She swooped into the morning sky without a sound. "We can start by finding the seagulls, and stopping this war once and for all."

The three SkyTalons took the long way around the tribe. They were careful to avoid being spotted by anyone as the blue jays busily worked to repair the camp.

Cornelius felt dread flood through him as they finally flew past the camp's borders and headed into the territory beyond. The last thing he wanted to do was see another seagull right now. In fact, he never wanted to see another seagull again. Even though Cornelius knew that this group of seagulls had nothing to do with the ones who had lived in the city all of those years ago, he still couldn't help but be reminded of them. The memories were still so strong... still so painful to relive. Cornelius instinctively glanced down at his side, let out a heavy sigh, and forced himself to focus on what was going on now. He glanced over his shoulder to make sure they weren't being followed.

"This is something that we must do alone," Shadow had explained before they left the Life Tree island behind. "The tribe is furious with the seagulls. If they knew that we were going to speak with them, they would see it as an opportunity to seek revenge and attack. But we aren't looking for a fight. We're looking for a peaceful solution to everyone's problems."

Now, Cornelius let out a sigh. This just didn't feel right to him. The seagulls obviously didn't seem as though they wanted peace, especially after they had just raided the tribe in the middle of the night. But Cornelius trusted Shadow completely. If this is what she thought was the right thing to do... than so did Cornelius.

Dustin suddenly halted, and he pulled himself into a hover. His eyes were wide with fear. Cornelius froze, coming to the same realization that Dustin had. The SkyTalons had left the safe borders of the Blue Jay Tribe, and were now in enemy territory. *We left without telling anyone,* Cornelius thought. *So if anything goes wrong, no bird would think to look for us all the way out here.*

Shadow began to hover as well. She kept her head held high, scanning the forest for any trace of the seagulls. She wasn't worried in the slightest, but Cornelius just couldn't bring himself to feel the same way. "Shadow," he began quietly. "I don't think we should do this. We should go back, while we still can-"

An ear-splitting cry suddenly tore through the silence, cutting Cornelius off. A huge seagull burst through the cover of some leaves and flew toward the three SkyTalons. While Dustin and Cornelius recoiled and shrunk backward, Shadow remained still. She watched the seagull approach unblinkingly.

The seagull hovered a feather's length in front of her, his gaze calculating and fierce. "Why have you come here?" he demanded. His yellow eyes slowly shifted from her, then to Cornelius, and then finally rested on Dustin. They suddenly filled with anger. "You are not welcome here," he angrily spat at the blue jay.

Cornelius turned his attention to Dustin, watching to see how he would react to the seagull's comment. Cornelius blinked, surprised, to find Dustin staring at the seagull with challenge in his eyes. A tense moment passed, with Dustin and the seagull's gazes locked. Then, Dustin looked away, his eyes brightening ever so slightly. Cornelius looked at Dustin, confused. The seagull's eyes narrowed.

Shadow suddenly moved forward, blocking the seagull's view of Dustin. "We are not here to fight," she explained. "We only wish to speak with your flock in peace."

The seagull went silent for a very long time, thinking carefully about Shadow's words.

"No," he said at last. "I will not trust any birds that side with the blue jays. You're planning something, I can just feel it. You must leave now. I don't want to cause any more fighting than I have to."

Shadow remained still. "That's why we're here. To stop the fighting. We only want to talk, and to find a solution to everyone's problems. A solution that makes everyone happy."

The seagull blinked, looking conflicted. "Fine," he said at last. "I'll take you to our camp. But I'm warning you, if this is a trick, it won't end well for you." He suddenly let out a loud cry. Cornelius froze as a talonful of seagulls shot out of the cover of the leaves, surrounding the three SkyTalons on all sides. There was no way they could escape now. Fear fell down on Cornelius, and his heart began to pound. Dustin's eyes were dark as they stared at the seagulls, and he extended his talons, prepared for a fight.

The first seagull signalled for the SkyTalons to follow, and they were forcefully led deeper into the forest. Shadow's idea of a peaceful meeting suddenly became very, very terrifying.

# CHAPTER 10

"*Rogues?*" Ellagard repeated as she slowly extended her talons. Hot rage flashed beneath her feathers, and it scorched through her like a fire. *How dare they come back here, after everything they've done?* she furiously thought.

"Where?" Ellagard growled, turning to the black and white peacock. Her yellow eyes glowed with determination. "Just a few wing lengths from ocelot territory," she reported.

Ellagard felt her head whirl.

*First, Zander appears to me, and Khan comes and takes him right after. Then some rogues think they can come into our territory,* she thought, feeling her feathers beginning to bristle. She clenched her beak. *Whatever game Khan's playing won't work.*

Ellagard stood taller. She pointed to the patrol in front of her with a wing. "You five, come with me," she commanded.

They nodded.

Ellagard quickly looked away and then scanned the rest of the tribe. She hurriedly chose a few more Protectors, making sure to include birds that were either swift or strong. A balanced patrol was essential.

Ellagard was soon in the center of her chosen nine birds, ten including herself. A thought suddenly struck her. *Who will temporarily lead the camp while I'm gone?* she wondered, her heart beginning to race. She quickly looked around, and then let out a sigh of relief.

Cyprus was lingering behind the crowd. His green eyes looked around at the scene warily, and his talons shook slightly as if it was an effort just to stand. *He'll have to do. There's no other option,* she thought, drawing in a breath. "Cyprus will lead the tribe while I'm away. Go to him if you have any issues," she hurriedly declared.

Her brother's green eyes widened with surprise.

"Follow me!" Ellagard called, refusing to waste any more time. She couldn't help but feel a rush of excitement as she began to run, leading the patrol. This was finally her chance to get out of the camp and do what she loved.

As she ran, the black and white peacock suddenly caught on a burst of speed until she ran side-by-side with Ellagard. "What's the plan?" she asked.

"Drive them out, and make them feel our talons," she responded. The black and white Protector nodded, then she drew back to let Ellagard take the lead once more.

With every step they took closer, the clearer the sounds of a skirmish became. Screeches of fury and the rustling of leaves filled the air. Ellagard abruptly stopped, spreading her wings to signal for the others to do the same. They were now only a couple of wing lengths away from the battle.

Ellagard lowered herself until she felt her feathers brush against the ground. The rest of the patrol quickly copied. Ellagard sharply nodded up toward the tree branches. Half of the patrol immediately broke away. Soundlessly, they slithered up the branches. Ellagard watched in satisfaction as they quickly became hidden by the dense foliage. Ellagard flicked her tail feathers forward, and she and the rest of her patrol soundlessly advanced closer.

Ellagard's eyes narrowed as she peered through the bushes that hid them. Rogues and her tribemates were viciously clashing, and feathers were scattered all over the ground. *It's a good thing that black and white peacock and the rest of her patrol came back when they did,* Ellagard realized. If they hadn't, the tribe's original patrol would have been gravely outnumbered. *And now the rogues are the ones lacking in number,* she thought excitedly, glad that she had chosen as many birds as she did.

Ellagard drew in a deep breath. "Attack-"

Her cry was cut off as she felt something slam into her side. Ellagard quickly rose to her talons and then felt her blood run cold. Her patrol had been ambushed!

More and more rogues slid out from the shadows, instantly clashing with the nearest tribe bird they saw. Cries of distress exploded overhead, and the Protectors Ellagard had sent into the trees came crashing down, with even more rogues swooping down after them.

Ellagard let out a screech of defiance. *There may be more of them, but their determination doesn't even begin to compare with ours!* she thought determinedly. "Attack with everything you have!" Ellagard yelled, throwing her voice above the sea of noise. "Drive them out!"

Ellagard quickly scanned the battle and found a sky-blue and black peacock. He was slow as he clashed with one of her tribemates, but his blows were powerful. Ellagard could easily match his strength with her speed... as long as she didn't get caught in his talons.

Ellagard shot past the battling peacocks, narrowly avoiding their snapping beaks and slashing talons. She ran faster and faster until the jungle became a blur around her. Only once she was a feather's length away from the rogue, she sprung at him with her talons extended.

Ellagard winced, feeling the breath get knocked out of her chest as they collided. Sharp pain exploded through her. The rogue only stumbled backward by a few paces. Ellagard froze, feeling dread surge through her. *He should have tumbled halfway across the clearing!* she thought in horror.

The rogue's brown eyes flashed with amusement. "Ah, the tribe's new leader," he smoothly commented. "Let's see if you're truly worthy of that title." The rogue leapt at her.

Ellagard narrowly avoided his blow by a feather's length. She swiftly darted forward until she stood behind him. Ellagard immediately whirled around, preparing to spring on him. She leapt into the air with her talons outstretched.

The rogue abruptly turned, and for the briefest of moments they were face-to-face. Ellagard's eyes widened in terror. She saw her own horrified expression reflected in his eyes. He was faster than she had expected!

The rogue lifted a talon high into the air and then with frightening strength, slammed it into Ellagard's side. She gasped as she felt herself slam into the ground. Agony surged through her. But Ellagard refused to give up. The tribe needed her! With all of her strength, she slowly began to drag herself to her feet. The rogue placed a talon on her side and effortlessly pushed her back down again.

Disappointment flashed in his eyes. "Sad. I thought that with you as their leader, our path to victory would have been more... challenging," he murmured. Ellagard met his gaze fiercely. The rogue shrugged, and then rose his other free talon. Each pointed claw eerily sparkled in the dim light.

Ellagard felt her blood run cold.

He suddenly plunged his talon down toward her. Ellagard slammed her eyes shut, expecting it to meet with her at any second. But that second never came. A shriek exploded through the chaos, and Ellagard felt the weight get lifted off of her.

Ellagard quickly rose to her extended talons, prepared to drive away the rogue with all of the strength she had left.

Ellagard stopped dead in her tracks. It was the black and white peacock! Her yellow eyes sparkled in defiance as she drove away the rogue, one swipe at a time.

Ellagard glanced around and felt light with relief. Everywhere she looked, rogues were being driven out of the Peacock Tribe's territory. They were winning the fight!

The black and white peacock suddenly let out a cry of rage. She took an ambitious leap toward the sky-blue and black rogue, her yellow eyes sparkling in defiance.

Ellagard felt herself freeze in terror. "No!" she cried, running forward.

But it was too late. In the foolish move, the rogue took the opportunity to lift his talon into the air. He was about to use the same move he used on Ellagard! But this time he wasn't as forgiving. The rogue's eyes flashed with anger, and with a powerful blow, he slashed his talons down the black and white peacock's neck. Losing her balance, she fell to the ground with a sickening thump.

A furious scream escaped from Ellagard's beak. *That was a sick, cruel move,* she thought. She would never let the rogue get away with it! Just as she was about to intercept him, he turned tail and fled after his fellow rogues. Ellagard's patrol let out cries of victory. Some of her tribemates even began to chase after them, refusing to let the fight end so soon. "No, stop," Ellagard demanded. "The battle is over!"

Ellagard quickly rushed to the black and white peacock's side. Respect for the injured Protector flooded through her. *She saved my life,* Ellagard realized, shocked that this would have been her final fight if it wasn't for the Protector crumpled at her feet.

The black and white peacock winced in pain, but offered a weak smile as she looked up at Ellagard. "We won," she said shakily, triumph sparkling in her eyes.

Ellagard grinned. She liked her spirit. "What's your name?" she asked, extending a wing to help her rise to her talons.

The black and white peacock blinked. "Reyna," she told her proudly. "My name is Reyna."

# CHAPTER 11

A storm was beginning to brew. Cornelius flinched as a cold raindrop landed on his head, soaking deep into his feathers. Seagulls surrounded him and the other SkyTalons on all sides, and Cornelius knew there was no turning back now. They were being led further and further away from the Blue Jay Tribe, and into the dangerous world beyond.

He quickly glanced to his side. Shadow flew without a sound, her fluffy black plumage swaying slightly in the wind. Her head was held high, and her gaze was focused and collected. *She's not worried,* Cornelius realized, letting out a breath to steady his nerves. He couldn't help but feel slightly relieved. *If Shadow isn't nervous, then I have no reason to be either. The three of us are together. We'll be okay... I hope.*

Cornelius had to keep on reminding himself that they were only here to talk about peace. But it was hard to not imagine a fight breaking out. For a moment, memories began to surface of the seagulls back in the city, but he quickly pushed them away.

The seagull leading the patrol veered slightly to the side. His wingtips twitched slightly, catching Cornelius' attention. He immediately understood this to be some sort of signal for the rest of the seagulls. The massive seagull suddenly began to dive, and he quickly became a white speck amongst the forest below. The rest of the flock quickly followed, ushering the three SkyTalons to do the same. Shadow and Cornelius quickly exchanged a glance before following.

It felt strange for Cornelius to be so close to a seagull without his feathers immediately getting torn to shreds. *I barely know anything about them, other than how they almost drove out our flock for good, and how much it hurts when they attack you...* Cornelius remembered nervously, feeling his side with a talon. *But these aren't the same birds.*

A blistering wind rushed through his feathers, making his huge orange eyes water. Grey clouds had tightly gathered overhead, and with them came a swarm of icy droplets of rain. The forest below began to rise up to Cornelius, faster and faster, until the green foliage wrapped around him.

Cornelius blinked, finding himself on the other side. They were in the heart of the seagull's camp now.

Their home was shockingly similar to the Blue Jay Tribe's camp. It was almost a complete match. The only thing missing was the lake and the Life Tree, and, of course, blue jays. Seagulls were perched as far as the eye could see, their white shapes dappling the camp like snow. Cornelius felt his heart skip a beat. There were so many of them!

The seagull leading the group let out an ear-splitting call, flying further ahead before swooping toward a jagged boulder. The seagulls surrounding the SkyTalons began to slowly break up, only leaving two of the burliest looking seagulls to fly by their sides. "Follow us," one of them commanded. She fixed her piercing yellow eye on them for a moment before swooping toward the ground, with her companion immediately copying. *This is it,* Cornelius thought as he dove. *This is the beginning of the end, for better or for worse. And soon we're going to find out which one it'll be.* He forced himself to hold back a whimper.

Cornelius, Shadow and Dustin landed closely beside one another, each of their feathers practically brushing. Cornelius and Shadow both instinctively kept Dustin in the middle, in-between the two of them. Dustin was the youngest and the smallest compared to the other two SkyTalons, and they both knew that he was their responsibility. If anything happened to Dustin again, Cornelius didn't think that he would ever forgive himself.

Cornelius looked at Dustin nervously. The blue jay's gaze was clouded, and his feathers were ruffled slightly. He tore at the grass below with a talon, his grey beak beginning to clench. Something was defiantly on his mind, but what? Just as Cornelius was about to ask, a booming cry erupted through the forest.

Cornelius realized, startled, that the whole of the seagull flock had gathered around them. He looked around at them warily, feeling his head begin to whirl with thought. This just felt so familiar. The grey boulder up ahead, the group of birds surrounding him, the dense forest protecting the flock below. This camp, and the way the birds acted, were just like the Blue Jay Tribe! *But why?* Cornelius wondered.

The flock silenced the moment the cry filled the forest. All heads turned toward the throne-like boulder in the center of the camp. A seagull suddenly glided through the air, then landed on top of the boulder. He was huge and powerful. His sharp talons clicked against the rock as he took a step forward, then lifted his head. He gazed at the three SkyTalons calculatingly, remaining silent for a few moments.

"Bow before Jerimiah, the leader of our flock," one of the nearest seagulls demanded, glaring at the SkyTalons.

Shadow and Cornelius hesitated for a moment before slowly lowering their heads. Cornelius looked at Dustin out of the corner of his eye. To his horror, the small blue jay kept his head held high, eyes blazing with defiance. Cornelius felt dread pour over him. *Dustin, please!* Cornelius wordlessly begged. *Just do what they ask you. We can't afford to mess this up!*

A tense moment passed before Dustin clenched his beak and dipped his head. Anger blazed in his blue eyes like a ravaging flame.

Jerimiah took a step forward, his gaze locked on the SkyTalons, then slowly tipped his head to the side. "What a strange group of birds," he began, not mockingly, but with a hint of curiosity. "A pigeon far away from a city, a raven in the wrong forest, and... a *blue jay*." He spat those two words as though they tasted bad in his beak. "Hmm, it's clear what side you two are on," the leader said with an emotionless look at Cornelius and Shadow. He was silent for a terribly long moment. "What brings you three here?"

Shadow took a step forward. She lowered her head briefly as a show of respect for the leader. "It's true that we have come from the Blue Jay Tribe, but that does not mean we favour them over anyone else," Shadow began, her voice steady. Cornelius blinked at her. She sounded much more formal and detached than she normally did around Cornelius. Shadow continued on. "We are here only to seek out a peaceful solution to end this war before any other birds get hurt. A solution that would make everyone happy."

Hushed murmurs began to break out all around the camp, filling the air like the buzzing of bees.

"But why now, after we just raided their camp?"

"This must be some sort of trick!"

"We need to drive them away."

"Silence!" Jerimiah called, throwing his voice over the sea of noise. "Let them speak!"

Shadow gave him a grateful nod before turning toward the rest of the seagulls. "Yes, your concerns *are* valid. But what I say is the truth," she said. "We are here to settle this dispute, once and for all, without any talons."

Jerimiah's gaze darkened as the raven spoke. He suddenly looked bitter and angry. "And why now, after all of these years?" he asked, trying to keep his voice steady. "Not even years. Lifetimes!"

Cornelius froze. *Years? Lifetimes? I thought this war had only happened recently!* he thought, confused. Dustin dug his talons deep into the ground, his eyes becoming hooded and narrowed.

Shadow looked taken aback. She was silent for a moment, thinking carefully about her next words. "But this war only happened recently..." she murmured, confused.

Jerimiah bristled. "From your narrow, tribe-like perspective, yes. But from our perspective, we have been wronged for generations," he spat, beginning to lose control of his temper. "And now we've finally had enough, and are taking matters into our own talons!"

The watching seagulls began to yell out with fury. Their loud voices made Cornelius' ears ring. He felt a stab of fear, expecting to feel talons rake down his side at any moment.

Just as he was about to instinctively step in closer to Shadow for protection, he stopped himself. Cornelius couldn't allow the seagulls to see how scared he was.

Jerimiah continued on, his white feathers starting to flare. "Where the tribe sits now is where *our home* used to be, before you greedy tribe birds took over!" he growled. "That land had belonged to the seagulls for generations. It was a good home. We lived on the island that now hosts the dead, stone tree. But that tree wasn't always like that. It was beautiful once, and full of life. It had meant so much to us. But one day that... *creature*... came and stole the life from our tree, leaving it dead and grey."

Jerimiah scraped his talons across the boulder he stood on. "The next thing we knew, a flock of blue jays came and drove us out. For years and years, the seagulls were treated as inferior pests! That is why we chose to fight. All we want is our home back! And we *weren't* even the ones to raise the first talon. We aren't battle-hungry or vicious, despite what you arrogant tribe birds believe!" he screamed.

Dustin suddenly let out a yell of fury and anguish. He extended his talons, feathers flared and bristling. Cornelius hurriedly took a few steps back, shocked at the small blue jay's sudden change of demeanour. "Despite what we *believe*!?" the blue jay spluttered, his talons quivering. "You ruined my life! My mother is gone now because of you *monsters*, and all she was doing was defending the Life Tree! How dare you call yourselves noble, after everything you've done!"

Cornelius and Shadow stared at him in shock.

Jerimiah's eyes were wide for a moment as he stared at him.

Angry tears were beginning to soak into Dustin's blue feathers, but nonetheless, he kept his head held high.

A tense moment passed, no bird certain of what they should do next. The seagull leader suddenly looked remorseful.

"It was you then, wasn't it?" Jerimiah said with a frown. "We are sorry for what happened to you. We really are."

Dustin slashed his talons through the dirt. "If you're so sorry, then why did you do it in the first place?" he accused. "Why did you have to ruin everything for me? For *us*?"

Jerimiah looked hesitant for a moment before lowering his head and smoothing his feathers. "Because we didn't do it. We had no responsibility for the attack that night. There is a traitor amongst your tribe."

# CHAPTER 12

Dustin stood frozen for a moment, his eyes growing as wide as a full moon. He gave Cornelius and Shadow a worried, terrified look. Finally, after a few seconds, he whirled around to face Jerimiah. "You're a liar!" Dustin screamed. "Don't believe a word he says," he added to Cornelius and Shadow through a gritted, clenched beak.

Cornelius felt his heart begin to pound fiercely against his ribs. *It's Atticus and Elizabeth,* Cornelius realized. *They're the traitors. They have to be.* He suddenly felt sick. *How could they have harmed Dustin's mother? Their own family? They're much, much worse than I thought. If they were willing to go to those lengths to get what they want... what are they prepared to do to Dustin?* He wondered, horrified. *Is that why they constantly want to keep him close to them? So that they can strike whenever they see fit?* Cornelius took a protective step closer to Dustin, half-expecting Atticus and Elizabeth to spring from the shadows at any moment. He looked at his friend, worried for his very life.

But Dustin looked anything but worried. A terrible rage was ignited in his eyes. His blue plumage rose and fell with every furious breath he took. Shadow's eyes widened. She hesitated for a moment before unfolding a wing to gently place on his shoulder. Dustin glared at her with such anger that the raven froze. "Please, don't let your emotions get the better of you," she pleaded. "I know you're angry, and you have every right to be. But we can't afford to mess this up. We have to end this war, not cause more fighting!"

Dustin suddenly let out a chilling, slow laugh. It startled Cornelius, and he was surprised that the happy, constantly cheerful blue jay could have such a noise slither out of his beak. Something in Dustin's blue eyes seemed to have snapped. "Oh no, you're right, Shadow. This war *needs* to end," he snarled. Then, he slowly turned toward Jerimiah. "How about I end it *right now*?" he asked in an overly joyful, pleasant voice. "How about I make sure that no birds have to suffer like I did, and get their whole lives ruined for them? How about I make this flock feel the same pain and loss that I did? How about I stop this war once and for all, right here, right now? Doesn't that sound just *perfect*?"

"Dustin, stop," Shadow breathed, eyes brimming with concern. Her gaze flickered from Dustin, then to Jerimiah. The leader stood still, studying the scene carefully. "Stand down."

Without warning, Dustin flung open his wings. In a blur, he exploded over the heads of the stunned flock and collided into Jerimiah with a sickening thump. The leader was knocked backward by a few paces, but looked unharmed. As he watched the scene unfold, Cornelius felt terror coil around him. *What is he thinking!?* He thought, appalled. *Dustin's so small compared to Jerimiah, he'll never stand a chance!*

Jerimiah broke away from Dustin, his expression unreadable. Seagulls were beginning to fly to Jerimiah's aid, but abruptly stopped as their leader lifted a wing to still them. Dustin let out a furious cry, leaping at the towering seagull with all of the strength he had. Just as Dustin was about to land a blow, Jerimiah took a slight step to the side, making the tiny SkyTalon miss, stagger and almost fall off of the boulder. There was nothing taunting in the leader's eyes as he avoided

Dustin's talons time after time again. In fact, he actually looked sorry for the blue jay.

Dustin lifted his head as high as he could, then looked Jerimiah straight in the eyes. Tears suddenly began to fall from Dustin's brilliant blue eyes, and his whole body shook with emotion. "Why won't you fight back?" he choked out. Then, he quickly wiped away his tears with his wing. "Fight back!"

Just before Dustin could leap forward and continue the fight, Cornelius and Shadow hurriedly flung open their wings and rushed to the boulder. They quickly put themselves in between Dustin and Jerimiah—but it was no use. Dustin's small size allowed him to easily slip past his fellow SkyTalons.

Dustin leapt at Jerimiah, faster and stronger than ever before. For a moment, it looked as though Dustin might actually land a blow against the seagull's flank.

Jerimiah was grim for a moment. Then, at the last second, he took a step backward. He watched sadly as Dustin stumbled, then fell on the jagged surface of the boulder with a thud. Scarlet blood trickled from a small cut under Dustin's beak, faintly staining his blue plumage.

Silence hung over the camp.

Shadow rushed to Dustin's side. She quickly looked him over to make sure that he wasn't seriously hurt, then helped him rise to his talons. Cornelius watched motionlessly, stunned with disbelief.

Shadow turned to Jerimiah, opened her beak to speak, but then closed it as he lifted a wing to silence her. "I think that it would be best if you three return to the tribe," he slowly told her. There was nothing bitter or dark inside of the leader's yellow eyes. In fact, he looked nothing but upset as he watched Dustin wipe away more of his tears with a wing.

Shadow hesitated for a moment, looking torn, before reluctantly nodding her agreement. She gently ushered Dustin forward. With a final longing look at the rest of the seagull flock, she unfolded her wings and swooped into the icy, unforgiving wind. Dustin and Cornelius trailed behind her.

*How can we leave now?* Cornelius asked himself in disbelief as they left the seagulls behind. *We were only just beginning to learn more about the Shadows Within... about Atticus and Elizabeth. And we were so close to finding peace and ending the war. But now we've lost our chance for both of those things. Will we ever get another chance again?*

Cornelius felt a stab of frustration as the three SkyTalons flew through the thick canopy of leaves, leaving the seagulls behind. With every flap of his wings, Cornelius knew that he was only getting further away from the truth.

# CHAPTER 13

Cold rain seeped from the grey and cloudy sky, soaking the forest and the three SkyTalons. Cornelius felt frozen, tired, and weak.

Shadow was silently leading the way back to the tribe. No bird had dared to speak ever since they had left the seagull flock behind. For the most part, their journey back had been soundless, except for the small sobs coming from Dustin. He had cried a few more times here and there, but Cornelius and Shadow didn't acknowledge it. *Shadow and I both know what it's like to grieve,* he thought. *And sometimes it's best to just have some time alone with your thoughts.*

Suddenly, thunder boomed in the distance.

Cornelius glided up to Shadow, blinking the cold rain out of his eyes. "We still have a long way to go," Cornelius began, looking at the churning lake far in the distance. Wind rushed through his drenched feathers. "Maybe it's best to rest until the worst of the storm has passed..." Secretly, Cornelius wanted to keep Dustin as far away from Atticus and Elizabeth as he could. *Don't worry,* he wordlessly told Dustin as he flew beside him. *I won't ever let them hurt you... not again.*

Shadow shook her head. "We're almost there," she replied. "It's best to reach the tribe before the storm gets worse."

Cornelius wasn't so sure.

Suddenly, Dustin flew in between them, looking blankly ahead. "I don't think I can fly anymore," he murmured. Cornelius felt a flash of pity for his friend. *He's been through a lot,* Cornelius realized. *He blames himself for the Life Tree being damaged. Then, he had to face the seagull flock and Jerimiah, the birds who might be responsible for the loss of his mother. I don't blame him for wanting to rest for a bit.*

Shadow eventually gave a reluctant nod, forcing her gaze away from the lake in the distance. Then, she dove downward to the cover of the trees below. Cornelius and Dustin followed, wind whipping through their plumage. In no time at all, the three SkyTalons found themselves on a branch under the cover of the leaves. They were sheltered now, for the most part. Other than the wind that wailed above the protection of the trees, the forest was silent. Cornelius listened carefully, catching another sound.

*Plop... plop... plop...*

Rainwater was managing to pass through the roof of branches above. It trickled down and gathered on a single, large leaf. Cornelius watched, amused, as every so often it would get so heavy with water that it would droop slightly, letting a single droplet escape into the forest beyond.

Cornelius turned his attention back to his fellow SkyTalons. Shadow was tearing at some loose bark on the branch underfoot, her eyes glazed with thought. Dustin sat motionlessly, his feathers fluffed out against the cold. He seemed to stare ahead at nothingness.

Cornelius suddenly began to feel very awkward. It was beginning to occur to him that Dustin and Shadow, his companions that he now shared a destiny and friendship with, felt like complete strangers to him. He wasn't sure why he was just realizing this now, of all times. But it began to nag at him nonetheless.

Cornelius turned to look at Shadow, then felt affection for her warm his freezing plumage. *We travelled so far and faced so many challenges together,* he remembered. *When times were, and are, hard for me, I can always look to her for support. And even though we went through so much together, I barely know anything about her. But one thing that I do know... is that I think I love her. More than she'll ever know.* Cornelius had to hold back a blush.

Then, Cornelius turned his head and looked at Dustin. *I feel like we're friends now... or maybe starting to become friends. But even still, I learned more about him from his angry outburst at the seagulls than through an actual conversation. But I still don't know much about him.*

Cornelius stared down at his talons. He thought long and hard about what he should say next. It felt like a good time to get to know his new friends better. The three of them might not get another chance to be alone like this. Not for a very long time, at least. "Do you guys ever feel strange about being some legendary SkyTalon?" was the first thing that Cornelius thought to say.

Dustin and Shadow turned and stared at Cornelius warily. They were silent for a long moment. Cornelius suddenly felt hot with embarrassment, realizing how dumb that must have sounded. "Sorry, that was a bad question. Can we start over?" he rambled.

Shadow suddenly looked nervous as she stared down at her talons. "I've never told anyone this before," she began shyly, "but I sometimes wonder if I'm even cut out to be a SkyTalon. For most of my life, I was told that I was a nobody. No bird believed in me, and no bird really wanted anything to do with me. So then when I found out that I have such a huge destiny, and that so many birds are counting on me, I was scared. This whole SkyTalon thing makes me feel a bit... self-conscious."

Dustin's eyes grew wide. "You? But you're so brave, confident, and smart! I wish I could be like that," he said. "My mother... she was the Speaker before me. And my father was, and still is, the tribe's leader. So my tribemates have always seen me differently, instead of just an ordinary blue jay like them."

Dustin's shoulders sagged. "Because of my parent's high statuses, everyone has always been... jealous of me. They always thought that I got some sort of special treatment," he murmured.

Dustin's eyes flashed with pain. "My mother was the only one who really stood up for me. She protected me, and she made sure that no cruel words ever reached my ears. But after she... left... I was all alone," he said sadly. "I heard my tribemates constantly whisper about me. Some of them didn't even try to hide how they felt about me. And after my father *forced* me into becoming a Speaker, and have a status that was one of the highest in the tribes, the bullying became a lot worse. There were so many birds who had longed to have the high position of a Speaker. And they were furious that it was given to me without a second thought."

Dustin sighed. "When my tribemates weren't taunting me over something I had no control over, they were ignoring me. I never had friends. Not until you two arrived at the tribe."

Dustin suddenly looked shy. "I haven't told many birds this before... but it's always been my dream to become a Healer," he said. "And it still is. I'd give all of my feathers to train as one."

Shadow looked surprised. "But being a Speaker is a great honour!" she exclaimed.

Dustin let out a nervous chuckle. "I guess it is, but I think it would be better if it wasn't forced onto me," he said. "I'd do anything to be a Healer, but Atticus has already said no, so it's too late for that now."

Cornelius felt a flash of pity and understanding for Dustin. His mind suddenly flew back in time, to when the seagulls in the city were still a threat. "I know how you feel. Before I was a SkyTalon, there were some birds who kept on attacking my flock." He didn't dare talk about or say the word 'seagulls' in front of Dustin.

Cornelius continued on. "The problems kept on getting worse and worse, and they just wouldn't leave my flock alone. It was terrible," he recounted with a shudder. "Eventually, my siblings, Jemma and Xavier, and I decided that we had enough. We were going to end the fighting, once and for all. I had gotten an idea, and we all agreed on the plan. So, the three of us snuck out in the middle of the night without telling anyone." As he spoke, he realized how the idea sounded more and more ridiculous. But it had seemed like the best choice at the time, and had ultimately been the decision that saved the flock and ended the fighting.

"We snuck into the heart of the bird's camp," Cornelius continued. "All we wanted to do was talk to the leader, and reason with her. But Xavier had other plans, and he attacked her. Birds swarmed us, and we became surrounded. There was no way out. A bird had grabbed me. It was me, or our flock. I told Jemma and Xavier to leave me. They refused. I..." he trailed off, gripping his side with his wing.

Dustin and Shadow gazed at Cornelius nervously.

Cornelius drew in a shaky breath, closing his eyes for a moment. "Sorry, I got a bit carried away," he said, forcing on a smile. "Since it was my idea, smart or not, to sneak into the bird's camp, I was viewed as the one who saved the flock. But really, Xavier was the one who fixed everything. But it didn't matter. I was the hero, and there was no changing the flock's mind. So they made me second-in-command, and I would be leader after my grandfather. Xavier was furious. He didn't like me much before... but after that..."

Cornelius shook his head, then turned to Dustin. He nodded sympathetically. "I know what it's like to have something forced on you, and I know how you feel." Dustin's eyes grew wide, as if he was surprised to have someone understand how he felt.

"What was it like to live in the city?" Shadow cautiously asked Cornelius. "I've only ever seen it from a distance..."

The three SkyTalons continued to speak together for hours, even after the storm had passed. And with every exchange, Cornelius felt the three of them growing closer and closer together as friends. There was so much that the three SkyTalons had in common that Cornelius never would have even begun to guess.

Now, the sun was warmly glowing. It cut through the darkness of the storm and dappled the forest below with its light. Everything seemed peaceful and calm. And for just a moment, as he continued to chat with his two best friends, he forgot about his worries.

But that moment didn't last long. The leaves violently shook overhead, and a distressed cry tore through the silence. Shadow jumped to her feet, her talons extended and ready for the first signs of danger.

Alessandra suddenly swooped down and skidded to a halt, landing beside the three SkyTalons. Her eyes were wide with dread, and her feathers were ruffled from panic. "You three have to come! Quickly!" she gasped.

Cornelius remembered how she had been on the patrol that first discovered Shadow and him in the forest. That had been right after they were attacked in Jajarii, and lost Dustin.

Alessandra had seemed shy and reserved then, so seeing her so distressed now made Cornelius feel uneasy.

Shadow's eyes filled with worry, and she rushed forward to the blue jay's side. Cornelius remembered how he had often seen Shadow and Alessandra go on patrols together, and would constantly have friendly conversations around the camp.

Dustin and Cornelius gathered around the trembling birdess. "What happened?" Dustin asked nervously.

Alessandra's eyes suddenly filled with tears. "It's the Life Tree," she sobbed. "Somebody has damaged the Life Tree!"

# CHAPTER 14

"It's awful," Alessandra cried, her voice shaky. "Whoever did this was *merciless*. They demolished a few branches before some Protectors spotted them. We don't know who, or what, they are." By now, her talons were shuddering from fear, but she forced herself to continue on. "The bird looked like they were covered in *shadows*, and they wore it like some sort of dark coat of feathers. Before the Protectors could stop them, the bird just... vanished. In the blink of an eye. They didn't leave a single trace of their presence behind!"

Fear surged through Cornelius. *It's just like how Atticus or Elizabeth attacked us in Jajarii,* he thought. *But I never realized that they had any power like that in the outside world.* He took a step closer to Alessandra. "Where was Atticus and Elizabeth during all this?" he demanded. Although Cornelius was next to positive that these two birds were the Shadows Within, he had nothing yet to confirm his suspicions. Dustin tipped his head to the side, glancing at Cornelius questioningly. Then, Dustin turned to stare at Alessandra.

Alessandra opened her beak to answer Cornelius' question. Then, she abruptly froze. Her eyes glazed with confusion, and she touched a wing to her head. She was silent for a few moments. "I... I don't remember," she answered at last, puzzled. "Why don't I remember?"

Cornelius froze. *She looked like she knew something for a moment there,* he realized. *How come she suddenly forgot?* A dark thought abruptly struck him. There was no telling what sort of abilities Atticus and Elizabeth, the Shadows Within, had. Could one of those abilities include manipulating the thoughts of birds that could potentially interfere with their plans?

Cornelius suddenly felt dizzy. Dustin blinked at him, looking concerned. "Are you alright?" he asked with a frown. Cornelius forced himself to nod at Dustin, then turned his attention back to Alessandra.

She had buried her head in her wings. "It's chaos in the tribe, SkyTalons," she murmured. "No bird knew where any of you were. Everyone thought you were captured... or worse. I begged Commander Myra to send out a patrol to look for you, and she refused. But I didn't give up, and I went out on my own. I knew I would find you. I knew that you three could fix the Life Tree." She lifted her head, her eyes glowing with the faintest spark of hope. "You saved Dustin from Jajarii, not too long ago. And everyone had thought that it couldn't be done. The SkyTalons did the impossible, so I know you can do it again. Come back and save the Life Tree. It has to work! You three are the only ones who can do it."

Dustin looked doubtful. "We can try, and I'd be willing to. But the Life Tree is different from me," he explained. "It's full of Jarquanzila's power and magic. I'm just an ordinary bird. This won't be an easy task. I don't think any bird has ever tried to repair a Life Tree before, so we can't be certain of what dangers will arise."

Shadow paused, thinking carefully about Dustin's words. "I am prepared to take a risk," she declared. "If we lose this Life Tree, then every other tribe's Life Tree would fall as well. We can't take that chance.

I say we try. But I won't do anything unless the three of us are in agreement. Cornelius, what do you think?"

Cornelius felt his heart sink. Of course he was willing to try. But how could he, knowing that this could put Dustin and Shadow, his best friend and the love of his life, in danger? But was it wrong to refuse, when the fate of every tribe relied on his agreement? Cornelius sighed. *Yes, it would be wrong,* he told himself. *The Life Trees, and the five tribes, are more important than any of us. And who knows, maybe this isn't as dangerous as Dustin predicts. Oh, Jarquanzila help us.* "Yes," he said at last. "I'm willing to try."

Shadow nodded. "Then we're all in agreement," she announced. The raven turned to Alessandra. "Lead the way."

Alessandra's eyes sparkled with relief. Wasting no time, she threw open her wings and took off into the chilly sky, leading the way back to the tribe. The three SkyTalons quickly followed. Wind whipped through Cornelius' feathers as he flew. Worry wormed beneath his plumage as he thought about all of the ways that this could go wrong.

*"Don't worry, Cornelius,"* the faintest voice murmured in the pigeon's head. *"You cannot save the Life Tree. And soon, it will be lost to history... just as you will be."*

Alessandra was right. The camp was in chaos. Blue jays were scattered everywhere, scrambling from place to place. It was as if no bird seemed sure on what they should do next.

Commander Myra stood in the center of the turmoil, her feathers flared. She was attempting to throw her voice over the sea of frantic words, but no bird seemed calm enough to listen to her orders. As Alessandra and the three SkyTalons glided into the camp, Myra's eyes hardened and narrowed, and her beak clenched.

Cornelius' heart began to pound. *Where is Atticus?* He wondered. *And why is Myra the one giving out orders in his absence?* As he scanned the camp below, he realized that Elizabeth was nowhere to be seen as well. Fear pulsed through Cornelius, and the air around him began to feel thin.

The Life Tree looked terrible in the distance. The once proud tree was cracked and damaged in several places, and broken branches littered the island. A cloud of dust filled the air, making Cornelius gasp and splutter. Dustin looked grim as he took in the miserable sight. But luckily, there were still many surviving branches on the Life Tree. Cornelius let out a sigh of relief. *Even if we fail, the tree will still live on... as long as it doesn't get damaged again,* he thought.

As the blue jays caught sight of the SkyTalons, they let out cries of joy and relief. Hope immediately filled the tribe.

"We're saved! The SkyTalons are here!"

"They'll know what to do."

"Things will be okay!"

Cornelius shrunk in his feathers. *They all believe in us,* he realized, worried. *How will they react if we fail? Will they still believe in us then?*

As they approached the Life Tree island, Alessandra abruptly halted, pulling herself into a hover. Cornelius blinked at her, confused. "All birds who are not Speakers or SkyTalons are forbidden to go near the Life Tree," she explained. "This is something that the three of you must do alone. Trust in yourself, and you will know what to do." And with that, Alessandra turned around and glided down to join the rest of the watching tribe.

Dustin and Shadow watched her go for a moment before resuming their flight to the Life Tree. Cornelius held back for a moment, letting out a gasp. Something was wrong. A headache was beginning to slither through his skull, and icy talons curled around his chest, making it hard to breathe. He shuddered, as if a frozen drop of water was sliding down his spine. Dread washed over him. The darkness was back. And that could only mean one thing: Atticus was near!

Fear exploded through Cornelius. What would Atticus do when he caught up to the SkyTalons? Would he stop them from trying to save the Life Tree? Would he finish them off, once and for all? Cornelius felt a flash of defiance. *No!* he thought. *Elizabeth and him will never hurt my friends again. They'll have to go through me, first.* Suddenly, he felt terrified. *But what if I'm not enough? What if he gets past me and reaches Dustin and Shadow?* There was only one bird that could protect the SkyTalons now... Jarquanzila.

Fighting past the wave of darkness and horrible pain, Cornelius forced himself to fly as fast as he could. Shadow and Dustin had already landed on the Life Tree island, and were looking at Cornelius questioningly. *I can't let them know something's wrong,* he told himself. *It might distract them from the Life Tree... and from reaching Jarquanzila.*

The world had blurred into two as Cornelius stumbled to a halt, landing on the Life Tree's pebble-filled island. The darkness was growing stronger by the second. He knew that time was running out. "Come on," he gasped to Shadow and Dustin. "We have to hurry."

Every step took Cornelius a great effort as he dragged himself to the trunk of the Life Tree. After what seemed like a lifetime, all three SkyTalons reached out a wing to place on the trunk of the grey tree. "Close your eyes and focus on the tree's energy," Dustin murmured, his voice distant as he concentrated. "Once we're inside of Jajarii, we should be able to repair the tree."

Cornelius started to feel sick. The darkness was just so much. Just so overwhelming. He didn't know how much longer he could stand it. He desperately reached out for the Life Tree's energy. But no matter how hard he tried to connect to it, he was still unable to reach Jajarii. He turned to look at Shadow and Dustin. They looked peaceful, as if they were sleeping. They were inside of Jajarii now.

Cornelius felt a stab of panic, the realization crashing down on him. *They were able to reach it because they're real tribe birds, and I'm just some pigeon in a place where he doesn't belong.* The darkness was as strong as ever now. Cornelius let out a gasp, then crumbled to the rocky ground. Fear fiercely gripped him.

*This is it,* he thought, petrified. *This is the end.*

Suddenly, the hissing of the waves in the distance silenced into nothingness. All feelings of darkness lifted off of him in a matter of seconds. The world around him disappeared into a black nothingness, and the only sound Cornelius could hear now was his own shaky breathing. *Jajarii!*

"I warned you, SkyTalon," Jarquanzila's voice hissed. "I brought back Dustin, and now you must stand on your own."

Without warning, Cornelius was thrown back to the outside world. The abrupt sounds of the howling wind and the crashing of waves exploded through his ears, making Cornelius flinch. In a daze, he glanced up at the Life Tree. It was still as damaged as ever. The SkyTalons had failed, and every bird in the tribe knew it.

Agony tore through Cornelius with unforgiving strength. The darkness was as strong as he had ever felt it before. Something sharp suddenly gripped his shoulder, digging deep into his flesh. Cornelius was roughly pulled to his talons and was yanked away from the Life Tree. Terror coiled around Cornelius as he found himself gazing into the furious eyes of Atticus.

# CHAPTER 15

Atticus' pale feathers rose and fell with every sharp, furious breath he took. There was a horrible rage in his eyes, one that made his hatred for Cornelius clear.

Cornelius instinctively looked for Dustin and Shadow for support, then let out a gasp. They were nowhere to be seen! *Oh no*, Cornelius thought, horrified, as he began to take a few steps backward, away from Atticus. *No, no, no! My friends! Where are my friends?!* A dark thought struck him, almost bringing Cornelius to tears.

"Tell me you didn't hurt them," he begged. "Please tell me they're safe. Please... please..."

Atticus' icy eyes narrowed into slits. A bone-chilling wind exploded past the two birds, causing the leader's feathers to lash. Black waves slapped against the jagged island, sending ruthlessly cold droplets of spray to land on them. But Atticus didn't flinch. His full attention was locked on Cornelius.

"After all of this time, after all of this pain that you caused me, the only thing you care about is *them*?" Atticus snarled, his voice like dripping icicles. He took a step forward.

Cornelius let out a warning cry. He realized in that moment that he was the only bird standing in Atticus' way, blocking his path to the Life Tree. "Stay away from it!" he demanded in a trembling voice.

Atticus' eyes suddenly became hooded, and his whole body shook slightly from his rage. "Why?" he spat. "Worried I might break a branch or two?" He slowly extended his talons.

Every instinct Cornelius had screamed for him to recoil, but he forced himself to hold Atticus' gaze. If Cornelius showed any sign of weakness, put a single talon out of place, he would be done for, and Atticus would destroy the tree. *I can't fight him on my own,* Cornelius thought. *I'll stall for as long as I can, until some bird comes to help.*

"I understand you now," Cornelius began, trying to keep his voice as steady as he could. "You resent the Life Tree so much, to the point that not even your own mate could have held you back from destroying it. So you ended her life, making sure that she wouldn't get in your way again."

Atticus' gaze darkened.

Cornelius continued on. "Then, you forced Dustin, your own son, to be a Speaker. You knew that he was young and inexperienced. He wouldn't be able to put up a fight when the time was right for you to strike again, like any other bird could have," he said. "And that's why you always kept Elizabeth close to Dustin. To make sure that he couldn't somehow escape the tribe and ruin your plans."

Cornelius glared at Atticus, disgusted with him.

"After that, you launched the first attack on the seagulls, creating a war with them and the perfect distraction. While everyone was busy, you could swoop in and destroy the tree even further! Everything is *your* fault! You are the traitor! You are the Shadow Within!"

Atticus suddenly leapt at Cornelius, knocking him to the ground. "How dare you insult me?" he yelled, voice twisted with rage. "How dare you accuse me of things that I never even did!?" Suddenly, something in his eyes snapped. "Oh, but I know why," he growled. "Because you're just like *him*. I saw it in your eyes the first day you arrived here in the tribe. You saw me as the enemy. You saw me as a threat. You saw me as nothing more than a villain!"

Cornelius held his breath as Atticus began to circle him like a ravenous wolf. "I was always the one blamed!" he shouted, anger oozing out of every word. "Every *little* thing that went wrong was *constantly* my fault. He scolded me like I was a hatchling. He scolded me like I was below him. And while *I* was the one keeping everything in one piece, *he* was the one basking in the glory for things that he didn't even do!"

Atticus let out a hiss of frustration. "Even the first day we met, he ridiculed me. *'Pfft, you? You hardly seem like the heroic type!'*" As he recalled those words, Atticus scornfully raised the pitch of his voice, mocking the speaker. "He always tried to put me down. Always called me a *traitor*!" he spat.

Then, Atticus slowly turned his loathing, infuriated glare onto Cornelius. "I see it runs in the family."

Cornelius gasped. The realization struck him like merciless talons. "It was my grandfather, wasn't it?" he whispered, everything suddenly making sense. "...Donovan."

Atticus flinched, as if hearing that name again after all of these years hurt him. "Oh, Donovan's a grandfather now, is he?" Atticus growled. Then, he suddenly laughed. And laughed some more. "Well, isn't that just hysterical?" Atticus sneered. "The very thing Donovan left the tribes for had to come back here and fix his mistakes! What a joke."

Cornelius shrunk in his feathers, feeling dread pour over him. "What are you talking about?" he choked out. "What do I have to do with him leaving?"

By now, Atticus' whole body was shaking from his emotions. "Everything!" he yelled. "You, and every one of your family members, ruined everything! It's because of *you* that Khan rose to power! It's because of *you* that Ellagard and I had to stop being SkyTalons! It's because of *you* that the tribes are dealing with this war! If Donovan had only stayed like I *begged* him to, life would be better for everyone. But no! He wanted to leave, right when we had a chance to defeat Khan, and go raise a family! He left us all to live a perfect, happy life filled with *smiles* and *laughter.*"

Angry tears suddenly fell from Atticus' eyes. "And guess what? After all of those times when he mocked me and called me a traitor, he was the one to actually betray us," he murmured. "It's funny, looking back at how much I admired Donovan and wanted to be his friend. I was so hurt when he called me those things, I thought I could never experience more pain than that. But, after he left us... left me... for good, not even turning back once, I knew that I was wrong."

Cornelius was silent for a long time, at a loss for words. Then, he slowly walked over to Atticus and gently placed a wing on his shoulder. "I'm so, so sorry," he whispered.

Atticus suddenly tensed up. He roughly slapped Cornelius' wing away from him, wiped away his tears, then put his fierce expression back on. "Listen carefully," Atticus demanded. "I am *not* the Shadow Within. And neither is Elizabeth. We are protective of Dustin because he is the only thing we have left of his mother."

Cornelius felt those words hit into him like jagged boulders. Everything he knew, or thought he knew, came crashing down in a matter of seconds.

Atticus continued on. "I can tell that you're searching for the real Shadows Within as much as I am. I'll tell you one thing: *stop*. You are getting caught up in something that you do not understand," he said. "If you continue down this path, you'll meet the real Shadows Within, and you'll be dead before you can even realize your mistake."

Cornelius felt frozen to the spot. Atticus glared at him for a very long time. "If you're smart, you'll stay out of my way from now on," he spat. Then, Atticus took off into the stormy sky, leaving Cornelius all alone with the half-destroyed Life Tree.

# CHAPTER 16

Ellagard gazed across the camp in apprehension. It had been a couple of hours since her, and the patrol, had finished their fight with the rogues. They had taken Reyna, the black and white birdess who had been injured during the battle, to the Healer's section of the camp the moment they had arrived.

Now, Ellagard felt a pang of nervousness as she tore at the grass underfoot. *I hope Reyna will be okay,* she thought. *She saved my life. If it wasn't for her, I wouldn't be here right now.* The thought terrified Ellagard. What would have happened to the tribe? They would have been leaderless, and the rogues would have known it. Ellagard quickly shook the thought away.

*It didn't happen, and I owe that to Reyna,* she told herself.

The camp around Ellagard was serene. The sky was a bright blue, and there wasn't a single cloud in sight. Sunlight beamed down onto the tribe, washing Ellagard's feathers with its warmth. A group of hatchlings bounced by her, sending their shrieks of delight into the air. Ellagard watched with a twinge of amusement as a huge, orange butterfly lazily bobbed through the camp, causing the hatchlings to scurry after it.

The tribe, for the first time in a very long time, seemed to be at peace. But not for Ellagard. There was still so much to worry about. *I won't relax until we drive away every single rogue from this jungle!* She fiercely thought. Then, she let out a sigh. *And not until I know that Reyna will be okay.* Guilt made her feathers seem heavy. Reyna shouldn't be the one getting treated right now. *It should be me,* Ellagard thought.

*I've been putting it off for too long,* she told herself. Although Ellagard wasn't good with sappy, heartfelt speeches, she knew that she had to go and thank Reyna. Ellagard owed her so much.

Ellagard hesitated for a moment, running through all of the ways she could embarrass herself, before rising to her talons. Then, she began to walk toward the Healer's section of the camp. As she passed them, her tribemates greeted her with a hint of uneasiness in their voices. It was as if they were nervous to be in their leader's presence. Ellagard felt her heart twist. *I wish they wouldn't think of me like that,* she thought. *Just because I'm leader now doesn't mean I'm above them. I'm still the same Ellagard that I was a few weeks ago... the one they weren't so freaked out with.* Ellagard sighed.

Suddenly, Ellagard felt a spark of joy as she spotted her sister, and the head of the Healers, Amara. The white peacock's head lifted as Ellagard approached, and her eyes filled with warmth. "Oh, so the great and powerful leader has time for her sister now, does she?" Amara teased. The two sisters hugged. Ellagard felt a flash of gratitude for Amara. *At least one bird still sees me as the same old Ellagard,* she thought, relieved.

Amara smiled. "But I think the real reason you're here is to see that one Protector," she said. "Reyna, right?"

Ellagard nodded, feeling a flash of anticipation. "Is she okay?" she asked. *If Reyna, or any bird for that matter, got seriously hurt or worse because of me, I don't think that I could forgive myself,* she grimly thought. To Ellagard's surprise, Amara started to laugh.

"I think she's more than okay," the Healer replied. "Ever since she got here, she wouldn't stop chatting! I think she's trying to make friends with every bird who walks past her."

Ellagard let out a sigh of relief. "There's something that I need to tell her," she explained. "Can I go see her, please?"

Amara nodded, then led the way deeper into the Healer's section of the camp. Ellagard quickly caught sight of Reyna. Her white feathers stood out amongst the green foliage, and her yellow eyes were bright.

She was asking a plethora of Healer-related questions to a young trainee who had been tasked to stay with her. He looked exasperated as he tried to ignore her and sort his herbs at the same time. As he spotted Ellagard and Amara, he let out a sigh of relief, snatched up his herbs, and trotted off.

Ellagard and Amara exchanged a knowing, amused look. Reyna's head shot up as she spotted Ellagard. "Hi!" she exclaimed. To Ellagard's surprise, Reyna swiftly rose to her talons and walked over to greet the two sisters. *I thought her injury had been so much worse than it actually is,* she thought, confused. She eyed the spot where the rogue had struck Reyna, surprised to find it almost completely healed. In fact, there were only a couple of her white feathers missing.

*Why did I think it was such an awful wound? And why did Reyna seem so hurt?* Before Ellagard could think about this more, Amara suddenly let out a gasp.

"Oh, I almost forgot, I have to go and see Cyprus," Amara began. Then, she turned her gaze onto Reyna. "I'm so sorry. But I don't think that I can find the time to go for our walk today. You're going to have to stay under the watch of the Healers until tomorrow, before I can confirm that you're ready to return to your duties." Amara sighed. "There's just so much to do around the tribe these days," she huffed.

Ellagard blinked, watching the disappointment grow on Reyna's face. She immediately felt a flash of pity for her, knowing how boring it could be to be stuck with the Healers. "I could take her," Ellagard suggested, "and report in back to you when we're done." Reyna looked at Ellagard admiringly.

Amara's eyes sparkled with gratitude. "You would do that?" she asked. "Thank you, Ellagard, that would be a big help!" She turned around, her back facing Reyna and Ellagard, and searched the camp for Cyprus. "Just make sure that Reyna takes things slow. It's very important that, since after suffering from an injury, a bird is cautious and careful. All sorts of problems could arise when…"

As Amara continued to ramble on, Reyna lowered her head. "Want to race to the outside of the camp?" she asked mischievously, keeping her voice hushed so that Amara wouldn't overhear.

Ellagard grinned. "I'll meet you there," she teased. "Try and keep up!" Then, in a flash, the two peacocks took off.

Ellagard drew in heaving gasps as she struggled to catch her breath. Exhaustion gripped her as she watched Reyna through bleary eyes. She was a few wing lengths in front of her, heading toward the tree that they had decided would mark the endpoint of their race. With triumph sparkling in her yellow eyes, Reyna slapped the trunk of the tree with her wing. "I won!" she joking declared.

Reyna had been faster than she expected! "Because I let you win," Ellagard jokingly retorted, joining Reyna beside the tree.

Reyna giggled. "You'll have to give me more of a challenge next time, then!" she responded.

Ellagard smirked.

Reyna lifted her head and gazed up at the tree, her eyes growing wide. Ellagard followed her gaze, then let out a gasp.

The tree was huge! It stretched high into the sky, and Ellagard was sure that its topmost branches met with the clouds. Reyna let out a huff of amazement before walking toward the closest branch. After studying it for a few moments, she turned to face Ellagard, looking excited. "Hey, let's climb it!" Reyna exclaimed.

Ellagard looked at the tree warily. It was a long way up. "I don't know," she said slowly. "I've been away from the tribe long enough..."

Reyna suddenly hopped onto the branch closest to the ground, causing Ellagard to trail off. "We taught those rogues a lesson or two today," she began, extending a wing to help Ellagard up. "I wouldn't count on them being brave enough to return so soon!"

Ellagard hesitated, feeling conflicted. *Reyna's probably right*, she eventually decided. And besides, Ellagard had wanted to get away from her endless duties and do something fun for the longest time. This was her chance to do it.

Ellagard took Reyna's wing in hers, joining her on the branch. Together, they began to climb. With every jump and leap Ellagard took, the more she felt her worries melt away. She was happy... happier than she had felt for a very long time.

It took a while, but finally, Ellagard and Reyna made it to the top of the tree. Ellagard drew in a gasp of awe. The jungle below looked so small! The jungle's trees looked like ants at this height, and far in the distance rested the massive, churning ocean. It stretched as far as the eye could see. White stars peacefully glimmered in the indigo and dark-blue sky, and the moon hung lazily in the center of it all. A soft breeze rustled the leaves around Reyna and Ellagard.

"It's beautiful," Reyna gasped, her eyes wide as she took it all in. For a few moments, the two peacocks stood in silence as they gazed down at their home.

Finally, Ellagard spoke. "I never got a chance to tell you," she began, feeling awkward as Reyna rested her gaze on her. "Thank you for saving me back there. I owe you my life."

Reyna laughed. "You don't owe me anything, Ellagard," she replied nonchalantly. "You would have done the same for me, or for anyone who needed help." Reyna returned her gaze back to the view of the jungle, looking away. Ellagard quickly copied, feeling awkward. *Does Reyna really think so little of it?* she wondered. *She saved my life, and she's acting like it's just something casual.*

Reyna suddenly nudged her, breaking her away from her thoughts. "Well, since you insist on owing me something, I'll ask you a question," she began. "What's it like to be leader of the tribe? Is it as glamourous as birds think?"

Ellagard froze, suddenly remembering all of the stress that had been surrounding her for the last couple of weeks. "Oh, it isn't glamourous at all," she said, shaking her head. "I can't remember a time when I've been more stressed. Since I became leader, I've felt the pressure of caring for the tribe weigh down on me like never before. The tribe is looking to me for leadership. If I put even a single talon out of place, I risk everything, for everyone."

Reyna was silent for a moment, carefully taking in each of her words. "I guess I hadn't thought of it like that before."

Ellagard was silent. Silent for a very long time. A thought had come to her. *Reyna proved her loyalty when she saved me from that rogue,* she remembered. *Without her bravery, the tribe would have been leaderless right now. And who knows what would have happened because of that?* Ellagard shuttered, then pushed the thought away. *Reyna's wise and confident, and we seem to make a good team. I trust her, and I know that she'll make a good deputy.*

Ellagard looked at Reyna. "Would you like to join me in leading the tribe?" she asked at last.

Reyna's eyes grew wide, and then she broke into a fit of laughter. "I didn't think tribe leaders could have a sense of humour," she said.

Ellagard shook her head, feeling frustrated. "I'm serious," she replied. "You proved to me that you're worthy of being second-in-command. I think that you'd be great in leading the tribe if anything ever happened to me."

Reyna froze, looking shocked. "You're serious?" she whispered. Ellagard nodded. Reyna thought for a few moments in silence. Finally, her gaze brightened and she lifted her head in determination. "Then I guess you'll be stuck with me for a long time!" she joked.

Ellagard felt her heart soar. Finally, something seemed to be going right in her life. She had found a deputy at last!

# CHAPTER 17

Cornelius landed on the tribe's pebble-filled shore. Guilt made each of his feathers feel like heavy stones. Atticus' revelations swarmed Cornelius' head, making him flinch. He felt disgusted with himself. He felt ashamed of himself. He felt embarrassed to even show his face in the tribe. *It's because of me that Khan rose to power,* he realized, wincing as if the thought hurt him.

Then, he felt a flash of fury, and the sting of betrayal. *No, it's not my fault at all. I had nothing to do with any of this. The only bird who should be blamed is Donovan!* he told himself, only half-believing it. *He betrayed his friends. He betrayed the tribes. He betrayed me!*

Cornelius had to force himself from slashing his talons through the dirt. *I respected him with every feather I had on me. I looked up to him. I trusted him. But it's clear that he didn't feel the same way,* he thought, bitter. *He used me and tricked me, and now I'm the one forced to deal with his mistakes. He tossed me aside, manipulated me into leaving my home, just so I could fight his battle for him. Had I really meant so little to him?*

As Cornelius became lost in his painful thoughts, the thick layer of clouds had slowly begun to melt away, revealing a stunning red and orange sky in its place. The trunks of the trees around him were ignited in a blazing red outline, as if they were being gripped by the tiny talons of fire. Cornelius found himself wishing that he could sink away inside of his plumage. Donovan wasn't the only thing making him feel worthless and humiliated.

All around him, blue jays were politely avoiding him, taking pity on the not-so-legendary SkyTalon who had failed in front of them all. Their hushed whispers made Cornelius cringe as he overheard them.

"How come they weren't able to fix the tree?"

"And to think we believed in them."

"It's because one of them is a pigeon, I bet!"

Cornelius felt as insignificant as ever as he heard that last comment. *Maybe it is because I'm some unwanted pigeon,* he realized, miserable. *Dustin and Shadow could reach Jajarii, and I couldn't. Have I been slowing them down this whole time? Had this whole journey just been a mistake?* He buried his head in his wings, wishing he could somehow just disappear from every bird's sight.

Cornelius tried to hide the tears running down his cheeks from the gossiping tribe, but knew all eyes were on him anyway, no matter what corner of the camp he went to. So he let the tears flow. As he cried, Cornelius barely noticed the sound of flapping wings approaching him. He blearily looked up, and found Shadow and Dustin walking toward him through a blur of tears. For just a brief moment, he felt happy. "You're safe!" Cornelius exclaimed, wiping away his tears with a wing.

Shadow blinked. "Of course we are," she said. "Atticus only told us to leave the island. He said that he wanted to speak with you alone." She gazed at him curiously, but decided not to say anything.

Dustin sat beside Cornelius. His eyes were distant with thought, and he distractedly dug his talons in and out of the small pebbles underfoot. Cornelius blinked, feeling a twinge of sympathy for his friend. *He must be feeling as much as a failure as I am,* he realized. *Is it wrong that knowing I'm not the only one makes me feel a bit better?*

Shadow sat on Cornelius' other side. She was silent for a very long moment. She stared past the lake, which was glittering with countless red, orange and yellow sparkles, and at the damaged Life Tree beyond.

Then, Shadow released a heavy sigh. "So, what do we do now?" she asked.

Cornelius thought about this question, desperately trying to find an answer. But no matter how hard he thought about it, the more lost he started to feel. *I don't know what we should do now,* he thought. *Everything I thought I knew is wrong. Atticus and Elizabeth aren't the Shadows Within, I'm powerless when it comes to helping the Life Tree, and instead of being there for my friends, I'm only getting in their way. How pathetic am I?* Cornelius wanted to scream.

So, instead of answering Shadow's question, he told his friends everything. He told them how Atticus, Ellagard and Donovan had been the SkyTalons before them. He told them how his own grandfather had indirectly let Khan rise to power. He confessed about his incorrect suspicions about Atticus and Elizabeth, despite how awkward it was to do it around Dustin. And finally, he finished by telling them how it was his, and his family's fault, that Donovan had betrayed them all.

Cornelius' words were met by a grim silence. Especially from Dustin. If he had any new opinion or view of his father after hearing this information for the first time, he did an incredible job of hiding it.

Except for the slightest hint of bitterness in his eyes, the young blue jay looked emotionless.

Shadow thought carefully about what she should say next. She gently took Cornelius' wing in hers. "I know that deep down, you think that it's your fault that your grandfather left the tribes," she softly told him. "But please don't blame yourself, especially for another bird's actions. This is not your doing, Cornelius." Her eyes darkened with a sudden memory, and it was clear to Cornelius that she was thinking about her brother, Malik.

Cornelius gazed at Shadow affectionately, grateful to have a bird like her in his life.

"So if Atticus isn't the traitor," Dustin muttered under his breath, "who is?"

Cornelius paused, unable to give Dustin an answer. He had no idea of who the Shadow Within was now. He had been so sure, so positive, that it had been either Atticus or Elizabeth. But now...

"I still think that it's my father," Dustin continued on, his gaze darkening. "He's never been a bird that could be trusted. I wouldn't believe a word he says, if I were you."

Cornelius shook his head, remembering his exchange with the tribe's leader. *Atticus is cranky and mean, but he isn't evil,* he thought. *I could tell on the island that he wasn't dangerous or power-hungry like Khan or Malik, just frustrated like I am. And his story adds up. He isn't the Shadow Within, and neither is Elizabeth.* Cornelius had to stifle a groan. *But then who is? Out of every bird in this entire tribe, who could the Shadows Within possibly be?!*

Cornelius warily looked around the tribe, scanning each and every bird. The Shadows Within could be any of them. He could even be looking at them right now, without even realizing it. And that terrified Cornelius.

Behind them, the sound of rustling foliage suddenly filled the air. Cornelius turned and watched as a patrol of about five blue jays flew into the camp. Commander Myra was in the lead. She flew swiftly, powerfully, leading the way for the others.

Myra signaled for her patrol to break up before swiftly gliding down to land on the boulder that Atticus used to address the tribe. Blue jays began to gather around, looking up at the Commander eagerly as they waited to be sorted into a patrol.

Shadow watched the scene calculatingly, her gaze searching. Without warning, the raven abruptly rose to her feet and began to walk to the crowd. "Follow me," she said without turning around. Cornelius and Dustin exchanged a glance before trotting after her.

When the three birds arrived at the crowd, Myra suddenly stopped giving out orders. She greeted the three SkyTalons with an icy silence, her gaze narrowed. All heads turned toward the SkyTalons at once. Cornelius immediately felt self-conscious. Shadow, however, looked unphased as she met Myra's gaze. "We'd like to join some patrols tomorrow, please," the raven stated.

*We do?* Cornelius thought, surprised.

Myra forced a stiff smile and nodded. "Very well. You can join this," she pointed at a small group with a talon, "dawn patrol. Do *not* be late." Myra glared at them for a painfully long moment, then returned her attention back to the other Protectors. She continued sorting them as if nothing had happened.

Cornelius looked at the blue jays he got grouped up with, then felt the slightest bit relieved. They all looked as scrawny and weak as he was. *At least I won't get embarrassed in front of them,* he told himself. *But I wish they didn't look so nervous to have the three of us in their patrol. I don't want them thinking that we're some sort of mythical and legendary creatures, instead of regular birds like them.* In fact, almost every Protector was looking at them like that. Cornelius shrunk back in his feathers.

Shadow went over to the patrol and began to greet them. Cornelius and Dustin hung back, staring down at their talons awkwardly. They both weren't up to speaking with unfamiliar birds. They were tired, not only physically, but mentally. They both needed some rest.

By the time Shadow finished, the moon had risen into the center of the black sky. The forest was washed silver in its pale, frosty light. The raven said her final goodbyes for the night, then turned around and walked off into the darkness. She signaled for Dustin and Cornelius to follow her, and together the three SkyTalons travelled to a secluded, empty spot in the camp.

"What did you do that for?" Cornelius asked Shadow once they were far away from the other Protectors. "I-I don't know how to patrol! I've only done it a few times in the city, but that was so different from a whole forest."

Dustin nodded his agreement, looking worried. "I'm a Speaker, not a Protector. I've never done this before, either," he confessed, a hint of embarrassment in his voice.

"I understand your concerns," Shadow told Cornelius and Dustin. "But the only way we're going to find our traitor is to be amongst our traitor. Whoever they are, they must end up joining a patrol eventually. And one day, we'll happen to be in the same one that they're in. They'll slip up and reveal more than they intend to. And when they do," she looked up at the moon, determination glowing bright in her eyes, "we'll be ready."

# CHAPTER 18

The forest around Cornelius was peaceful and still as he slowly awoke. The sky was a happy shade of blue, and was dappled with a few small, fluffy clouds. A relaxing, warm breeze whispered through the camp, making the leaves around Cornelius flutter slightly. In the distance, the lake was calm as it rhythmically rolled up and down the shore. Its soft sound filled the air.

But, even despite this serene morning, Cornelius refused to let himself relax. This was an important day. He, and his fellow SkyTalons, needed to be sharp. They needed to be cautious. They needed to be ready. The SkyTalons could very well meet the Shadows Within today.

Cornelius was one of the first birds to awake in the tribe. He was eager to get started on today's patrols. The longer Cornelius waited, the more nervous he felt himself become. The sooner they exposed the Shadows Within, the sooner the Blue Jay Tribe would be safe once more. And then Cornelius, Shadow, and Dustin would move on to face their biggest, most dangerous challenge yet: defeating Khan.

Cornelius forced himself to push the thought away. The villainous, rogue peacock wasn't his priority right now.

Cornelius couldn't bring himself to rest on the tree's branch a moment longer. His talons were itching to start the day. He slowly unfolded his wings and glided down to the ground, careful not to disturb the sleeping tribe around him.

As Cornelius landed near the lake, feeling the soft grass beneath his talons, he began to worry. But this time his troubles weren't caused by the Shadows Within. *I've never done a patrol with a tribe before,* he remembered.

His thoughts suddenly flew back in time; to the last time he had done a patrol. That had been back when he was still living in the city. Cornelius smiled, remembering how he had accidentally slept in that morning and made everyone wait for him. His sister, Jemma, had woken him up, saving him from further embarrassment. *Jemma was always there for me,* he thought, feeling a pang of longing for his city home... for his family.

Cornelius would do anything to see them again. But they seemed like a world away from him now. Cornelius hung his head in shame, remembering how he had left them all without even saying goodbye. That decision still bothered him to this day, and with a bitter stab of anger, he remembered how Donovan had been the one to suggest such a terrible thing.

*Does Jemma, and the rest of my flock, still think about me?* he wondered, digging his talons in and out of the earth. *Do they even care that I'm missing? Should they?* He clenched his beak. *No, they shouldn't. I was just like Donovan. I left them all, only thinking about myself, and ignored how they felt. I don't deserve to be missed.*

Cornelius drew in a deep breath to steady his nerves, then forced himself to focus on the task ahead of him. The most important thing now was to find, and stop, the true Shadows Within. As thoughts began to swirl in Cornelius' head, a blue jay stirred. He watched as Alessandra glided down from the branch she had been sleeping on. She then landed a wing's lengths away from him.

Alessandra looked at Cornelius shyly.

"Hello," Cornelius greeted after a few seconds. He felt surprised with himself. For a moment, he had forgotten that Alessandra had been assigned to the same patrol as him.

She awkwardly smiled. "Hi," she said quietly.

A long moment passed. Both birds avoided meeting gazes, and they silently stared into the tribe, unsure of what to say or do next. Then finally, Alessandra spoke. "Thank you for doing your best to save the Life Tree the other day," she began. "I know that you three did everything you could, so don't blame yourselves. Sometimes Jarquanzila has his reasons for not wanting to help us. But it might be for the best this way."

Cornelius froze. *How does she know that Jarquanzila refused to help us?* he wondered, feeling fear slide down his spine like a cold drop of water. Just before he could question her, another member of the patrol swooped down and landed beside them, looking flustered to be in the presence of a SkyTalon. Cornelius felt a stab of annoyance. He couldn't question Alessandra in front of him.

Eventually, more and more blue jays, along with Shadow, joined the group. They were almost ready to head out on their patrol.

On the far side of the camp, Cornelius spotted Dustin walking toward them. He was closely followed by a fretting Elizabeth. "And remember, just because you're a SkyTalon now doesn't mean that you can't get hurt," Cornelius heard her tell Dustin as they came into earshot. Dustin sharply nodded, looking exasperated with his aunt.

Elizabeth saw this but continued on anyways. "You aren't a Protector, so if there's danger, make sure you fly away as quickly as possible. Leave the fighting to the more experienced birds. And then..."

Elizabeth trailed off when she spotted Cornelius. As she looked at him, frustration burned in her eyes. *Atticus told her about my old suspicions with the two of them,* he realized, feeling hot with embarrassment.

Dustin took the opportunity to break away from his aunt. "I'll be safe, I promise," he quickly told Elizabeth, then flew away before she got the chance to keep on lecturing him.

Elizabeth gazed at her nephew lovingly before turning around and heading toward the Healer's section of the camp.

When Dustin arrived, his mood brightened. He warmly greeted Cornelius and Shadow.

By now, every bird that had been assigned on this patrol had arrived. The blue jays were silent, keeping their heads low and gazes latched to their talons. Cornelius could tell that they were nervous about embarrassing themselves in front of the three SkyTalons.

An awkward moment passed. Eventually, a scrawny blue jay stumbled forward, gathering the courage to speak in front of the SkyTalons. His pale-blue feathers were ruffled slightly, and his lime green eyes sparkled nervously. "Um, hello," he began, fidgeting with a blade of grass. His voice cracked every so often as he spoke. "S-so usually Commander Myra leads us. But, since she's busy today with another patrol, we figured that you three could lead us, since you're the SkyTalons and all. But, you don't have to if you don't want to, of course."

He suddenly looked embarrassed. "Oh, I'm sorry, I forgot to tell you. My name is Nathaniel. But feel free to call me whatever you want." He cringed, realizing how dumb that may have sounded.

Nathaniel shrunk back in his feathers, as if he expected the three SkyTalons to burst out laughing at him. Dustin saw this, then gave Nathaniel an encouraging nudge. "Nice to meet you, Nathaniel," he said. A small, nervous smile appeared on the scrawny blue jay's face.

Shadow nodded, considering Nathaniel's words. "Yes, we could take the lead, if that's what you wish," she replied, earning murmurs of approval from the others. Shadow unfolded her wings and took off into the sky. "Follow me," she called to them over her shoulder, leading the way into the forest beyond the camp.

A soothing wind rushed through the patrol's feathers as they observed the territory from high in the sky. In the distance proudly stood the mountains. Cornelius stared at them in awe. It only felt like yesterday when, with Shadow at his side, he had crossed them.

Cornelius still felt nervous whenever he thought about the Raven Tribe, who lived on the other side of those great peaks. He knew that they were growing stronger, and more dangerous, every day under the vicious rule of Malik.

Cornelius quickly pushed the thought away. He was powerless to change anything in the Raven Tribe now. But, he could make a difference here, in the Blue Jay Tribe. *Don't lose your focus, Cornelius,* he told himself. *A Shadow Within might be only a feather's length away. If they show any signs of being a traitor, I can't afford to miss it.*

Cornelius scanned the patrol, analyzing each and every bird in turn. Nathaniel and Dustin brought up the rear, flying behind the others. They seemed to be chatting more than scouting for danger. Shadow was still in the lead. She was staring down at the ground, her gaze intense and focused. Shadow seemed as if she was scanning each and every branch in the forest.

Suddenly, the raven's gaze hardened. Shadow quickly pulled back and began to hover. Alessandra, Nathaniel, and the rest of the patrol quickly copied her. Cornelius nervously looked around, realizing that they had neared the border with the seagull flock. *But it's still a far distance away,* he realized. *We aren't even close to crossing it.* Cornelius eyed the forest floor below. *Why did she get spooked like that?*

Shadow gave a strange signal to the patrol with her tail feathers, stiffly spiking them out as if they had become flecks of stone. The rest of the Protectors shot one another looks of dread before they shot down into the cover of the trees below.

Cornelius blinked, puzzled. He exchanged a confused glance with Dustin before Shadow roughly ushered the two of them to dive down with her.

Cornelius felt his heart pound against his ribs as he landed on the branch beside the rest of the patrol. *What had Shadow signaled to them?* He wondered. *If only I had some sort of knowledge about Protectors.* Cornelius began to feel slightly embarrassed with himself.

*Wait, what is that?* Shadow did another signal, this time with one of her wings. She unfolded it, holding it out for a brief second, before slowly folding it in again.

Nathaniel was the first to obey the command. He lowered himself as far as he could go until he was pressing against the branch. It took no time at all for every other bird to do the same.

Cornelius held his breath. Slowly, as carefully and silently as he could, he peeked over the branch. A few of his grey feathers snagged against the rough bark, but his pain was nothing compared to his horror. Down below, far within the borders of the tribe, was a whole patrol of seagulls!

# CHAPTER 19

The seagulls slid carefully through the branches, surprisingly agile and silent for their massive size. Cornelius watched them, feeling terrified and confused all at once. *They aren't flying,* he thought, feeling his heart beat faster. *That can only mean one thing: they don't want to be spotted.*

Cornelius stiffened. What were the seagulls planning, and why were they here?

Cornelius quickly counted the white birds below, then let out a small sigh of relief. *We have more birds on our patrol than they do in theirs,* he realized. Worry wormed beneath his plumage. *But with their enormous size, will it matter if it comes down to a fight?*

As quietly and carefully as he could, Cornelius turned to look behind him. As he gazed at his companions, he began to feel nervous. It was clear that their worry mirrored his own. Their eyes were wide and bright with panic as they stared down at the seagulls.

Nathanial was violently shaking, terrified. Dustin was beside him, whispering words of comfort as he desperately tried to get him to calm down.

As Cornelius took in the pitiful sight of his patrol, a sudden feeling of fear exploded through his feathers, and the world around him began to spin. Cornelius tightly gripped his talons deep into the branch below to steady himself, causing it to splinter slightly.

Suddenly, Cornelius remembered last night, when Commander Myra had been sorting the patrols. *She had created groups that were* balanced with both experienced and training Protectors. *This is the one patrol that wasn't balanced. This is the patrol that Myra put us in.* Cornelius' head began to reel. Had Myra purposely done this, knowing that if anything went wrong during the patrol, the SkyTalons would be more likely to get injured—or worse?

Dread pooled over Cornelius' plumage. *Could Myra be one of the Shadows Within?* He wondered, the air around him suddenly beginning to feel thin.

Shadow suddenly stirred, so slightly that Cornelius had almost missed it. His attention immediately snapped back to her. *Myra will have to wait,* he told himself. *Right now, the one thing that we need to worry about is staying alive.* Cornelius watched Shadow carefully. He realized that her feathers were bristling. But it wasn't because Shadow was fearful or worried.

*It's another signal...*

Cornelius watched her, trying to make sense of her strange movements. Her black feathers slowly ruffled as much as she could make them. Then, she abruptly smoothed them down. She repeated this multiple times, and each time she did it, the more aggressive and quick the actions became. The raven's intentions suddenly became clear, even to Cornelius.

Shadow wanted them to attack the seagulls.

It would be the only way to ensure the safety of the tribe. The seagulls were motivated by vengeance, and there was no telling what the sneaking patrol would do if they were allowed to reach the blue jay's camp.

Nathanial let out a gasp of horror. The rest of the patrol looked just as terrified. Dustin and Cornelius exchanged a worried glance. Before any bird could question Shadow, she rose to her thorn-sharp talons and dangerously extended them, ready to fight. She drew in a deep breath, then tossed back her head.

"Blue jays, attack!" Shadow screeched. "Drive them out!"

Before the seagulls could react, Shadow exploded through the cover of the trees and barrelled into the nearest seagull with a thud. They crashed through the foliage, each bird trying to overpower the other. The tribe's patrol followed her, flying into a battle they knew they had a very slim chance of winning.

As Cornelius dove from the safety of the trees, he felt an explosion of terror rush through him. The trees around them violently shook, and an army of seagulls rushed into the clearing. Their numbers weren't only just enough to match the tribe's patrol; it was enough to exceed them.

*So that's what their plan was,* he realized. *This is an ambush!*

Blue and white feathers collided as the two opposing groups clashed. Dazed with fear, Cornelius accidentally allowed himself to get intercepted by a seagull. He winced as sharp, webbed talons dug into his feathers. He was roughly knocked off balance and was sent spinning to the forest floor. He crashed with a thud, feeling the breath get knocked out of his chest. Sharp pain surged through Cornelius. Just before he could rise to his talons, the seagull who had attacked him pinned him to the ground. She dug her talons into him. "I thought the seagulls called themselves peaceful!" he gasped, desperately trying to dislodge her.

The seagull let out a snort of amusement. "After so many years of suffering and pain, how peaceful do you expect us to be?" she spat. "We are tired of waiting in vain for some sort of acknowledgement from the tribe. So tired that we willingly partnered with one of the tribe's insufferable blue jays to finally get what we want." She let out a cackle. "To think that one of your own hates the tribes as much as we do."

Cornelius felt his heart skip a beat. *She's talking about a Shadow Within,* he realized. Cornelius let out a gasp. *She must know who they are, and what they look like!*

The seagull continued on. "Normally, we would refuse any sort of partnership with a *blue jay*," she spat out the name as if it tasted bad in her beak. "But when we heard their plan, it was too good to miss out on. That blue jay really hates every single one of you. We couldn't help but take a liking to them. And by working together, and by following their plan, we both end up getting what we want most: the destruction of the Blue Jay Tribe. We all win!"

Cornelius felt cold with dread. "But can't you see that they're using you?" he spluttered. The seagull frowned, but said nothing as she waited for him to go on. Cornelius carefully thought about his next words. This could be his last chance to uncover the true identity of the Shadows Within.

He wouldn't let this slip through his talons.

Cornelius struggled to think clearly with the battle still raging on around him. "I know that you have no reason to trust me, but I ask that you please listen," he began, struggling to throw his voice above the noise. "I understand that it's hard to be away from your home. I miss my home every single day, and I wish that I could see it again, even for just a moment."

The seagull gazed at Cornelius unblinkingly. He could tell that she didn't care. Thinking fast, he continued on. "I know that you want your home back more than anything, but partnering with that blue jay isn't the way to do it. They are cruel and dark-hearted, and just want to use the seagulls for their own gain," Cornelius said. "But once they're done with you, and they've gotten their revenge on the tribe, they won't give you your land back. There won't be *any* land to give back. This blue jay will end up destroying *everything*."

The seagull paused, carefully considering Cornelius' words. Something in her eyes suddenly softened. *It's working!* He realized. "This bird is dangerous," Cornelius pressed on. "They don't care about the seagulls. They don't care about their own tribe. And, they most certainly don't care about peace. I have been working to stop them ever since I came to this tribe. But I can't do that unless you help me." Cornelius looked straight into her eyes. "If you tell me who the blue jay is, I promise that I will do everything I can to stop the fighting and get you your home back."

The seagull went silent for a long time, looking torn. If she betrayed the Shadow Within, she could be throwing away her flock's last chance at getting their home back. But, if she let the blue jay continue on with their plans, her flock might not have a home to return to. The seagull drew in a deep breath. "Okay, I'll tell you," she said. "I don't know who you are, or if what you're saying is even the truth. But, for some strange reason... I trust you. For now. Please don't make me regret this."

Cornelius felt his heart pound. This was it. He was about to discover the identity of one of the Shadows Within!

"I think you might be close to them. I saw you together when we raided the tribe all those nights ago. Their name is-"

Dustin and Nathanial suddenly collided into the seagull, knocking her off of Cornelius. She tumbled backward by a wing's length or so, looking dazed. The seagull scanned the clearing, her eyes growing wide. Her flockmates were beginning to flee, flying away as quickly as they could.

The blue jays had won this battle.

As another seagull passed her, he let out a warning cry, urging her to follow the rest of her flockmates. The original seagull that Cornelius had been speaking to was by herself now. She was quickly becoming surrounded by the blue jays. Dustin glared at her for a very long moment, his eyes dark. She broke her gaze away from him, then shot Cornelius an apologetic look. "Please, remember your promise," she said, before unfolding her wings and flying away.

"No!" Cornelius screamed before he could stop himself. As she vanished into the forest, the blue jays let out cheers of victory. Cornelius hung his head, frustration surging through him. *She's gone, and so is my chance of discovering who the true Shadows Within really are.*

# CHAPTER 20

A half-moon hung lazily in the night's inky black sky, and was surrounded by countless glittering stars. Other than the soft lapping of the lake's waves in the distance, the night was silent and still. Not even a breeze dared to rustle the foliage.

But, despite this calm night, Cornelius felt nothing but frightened. Dark, dreadful dreams slithered through his head, making his heart pound in the waking world.

"No," he whispered in his dream, finding himself in the middle of the tribe. All around him, blue jays were flying as fast as they could. They all swarmed toward the main exit of the camp, each desperate to escape.

"Wait!" Cornelius called out to them. "We can help you. You don't have to flee. Come back!" His words were in vain. Not a single bird was paying attention to him.

Cornelius felt a stab of terror. Why were they all trying to escape the tribe? What horror could have caused this? Could it be the seagulls, back for revenge? Cornelius gulped. He looked around nervously, then felt fear strike deep in his heart. Cornelius drew in a shaky gasp, shrinking in his plumage.

It was a Shadow Within!

The traitor was perched, alone, on the highest branch of the Life Tree. Their black, shadowy wings were unfolded as they basked in the chaos and panic they had caused. They watched as the last of their tribemates fled into the night, satisfied, before gazing up into the starless sky. The shadow abruptly lifted a talon into the air, letting out a gleeful and triumphant cackle. Cornelius flinched as the shrill noise filled his ears. He suddenly felt sick as a familiar feeling of darkness gripped him. Cornelius released an agonized gasp, and he crumbled slightly. Pain surged through him.

The shadow continued to reach up higher and higher, unaware of Cornelius' presence. Moonlight shone onto each of their shadow-masked feathers, outlining them in a faint silver glow. *They want the moon,* Cornelius realized as he weakly watched the shadow try to grip it in their talons. The darkness was ravaging through him, stronger than ever now. *But why?*

The shadow paused for the briefest of moments to gaze up at it, their beak widening as they greedily grinned. Unlike in the waking world, the moon here was full, sparkling in its full power. The shadow wanted it all. The shadow needed it. The shadow must have it! They lifted their talon as high as it could go. It was as if they expected to pull the moon down toward them, just by its beams of silver light alone. Finally, they managed to hook their claws around the moon.

Cornelius watched in dread. Somehow, he understood that by the shadow having the full moon, they had won, and the SkyTalons had failed. All five of the tribes would fall.

The shadow rolled the moon around in their talons, looking pleased. Cornelius shivered. This bird was acting as if it were their plaything! The traitor stared down at the moon smugly, knowing that it was theirs now. Nobody could stop the Shadows Within now. Not even the legendary SkyTalons.

Suddenly, their eyes began to widen, and they let out a small gasp. Half of the moon was starting to vanish! It faded away, disappearing from sight in a matter of seconds. Cornelius blinked, realizing that the moon in this dream now mirrored the one in the waking world. "No!" the shadow screamed, their voice twisted with fear. They dropped the moon, horrified, and took a few steps back.

The dark coat of shadows that they wore suddenly began to slip off of their feathers, like mud in the rain. First, it vanished from their talons, and then their wings. The shadows slowly disappeared until only their face was covered. It pooled at their feet, now just a useless black puddle. The uncovered blue jay desperately tried to gather it back up again with their wings, as if it would somehow return to their plumage. But the shadows were vanishing fast. The black liquid trickled away from the blue jay, disappearing into the dark dream.

Suddenly, in their hurried scramble, they noticed Cornelius. The shadow let out a yelp of surprise, horrified to find another bird in their dream. Especially at the worst time for them possible. For a few moments, the two birds stared at each other, unsure of what to do next. Cornelius held his breath. The shadow abruptly let out a furious hiss. Just before the shadows on their face could melt away and reveal their identity, they turned their back to Cornelius. The blue jay tightly wrapped their wings around their face.

"Stay out!" they hissed, suddenly looking small and helpless. "Never come back here again!"

The ground began to violently shake and rumble, and the dream started to fade away into nothingness. Cornelius felt a shrill spike of horror. The blue jay was kicking him out of the dream!

"Wait!" Cornelius pleaded, watching as the blue jay shrunk deep into their feathers. *They're scared,* he realized, finding it slightly unsettling to see their blue feathers for the first time. Cornelius could tell, even with their face wrapped around their wings, that they were without the cover of any shadows now. *This could be my chance to put an end to this, once and for all.*

"Wait," Cornelius repeated as gently as he could. "Let's just talk. I'm not here to fight." To his surprise, the ground stilled and the dream stopped fading. Cornelius felt his heartbeat quicken. He had gotten the blue jay's attention. "You don't have to do this," Cornelius urged. "Whatever happened to you, whatever pain you're going through, I know that we can work it out. No more fighting. No more suffering. Please."

The blue jay was silent for a very long time as they considered Cornelius' words. "How did you get in here?" they demanded at last. They purposely made their voice sound strange and deep so that Cornelius wouldn't recognize it.

"I... I'm not sure," Cornelius answered honestly. He paused as a thought struck him. "But maybe things were supposed to happen this way," Cornelius began. "This could be our chance to work out a solution to both of our problems, in a way that we are both happy with. This... this could be fate."

The blue jay scoffed, the noise muffled from under their wings. "Fate is a cruel thing," they bitterly retorted. "Fate chose me to be the one who brings down the tribes. Fate made me suffer. Fate turned me into the monster I am." The blue jay drooped slightly. "That's why I'm doing this, Cornelius. To get back at fate... and the tribes. They ruined me. So now I'm going to ruin them. I'm sick of being trapped here. I'm sick of being reminded of what I've lost. If I never see the tribes again, it'll be too soon."

Cornelius blinked, surprised at the blue jay's words. "Then why don't you just leave?" he asked. "What's holding you back, if you hate the tribe so much?"

The blue jay let out a snort of laughter. "Revenge, of course," they growled. "I can assure you, I *will* leave. But not yet. Not until every single one of my insufferable tribemates regrets what they did to me. And once I'm done, there isn't going to be a bird left in this forest who isn't terrified of me."

They let out a slow, cold laugh. "I have to admit, it's also quite fun to be the villain for a change," they told Cornelius. "Seeing you scramble to figure out who I am, while I'm practically sitting under your beak, is hilarious. And this power of mine is amazing. It's just how I've always dreamed. I'm different from other birds, a one of a kind. And not only that. I'm *above* them now, too." Cornelius could tell that they were smiling from under their blue wings.

"When the moon is full in the waking world, I will become the most powerful bird in the entire world," the blue jay continued. "And anyone who stands in my path will be powerless to change a thing. You, and the tribes, will feel my wrath!"

Cornelius stood taller, pushing back his fear. "I'm never going to let that happen," he firmly stated. "I'm sorry that you're upset. I really am. But you can't take your anger out on the tribes. Sooner or later I *will* find you, and I'm going to put an end to this."

The blue jay cackled. With their wings still covering their face, they rose to their talons. "You'll put an end to this, will you?" they dangerously snarled. "Let's just see about that!"


Cornelius gasped, drawing in a deep breath. *They just kicked me out of their dream,* he realized shakily, finding himself back in the waking world. It was still as peaceful and calm as ever. He warily scanned the silent tribe, knowing that any one of the sleeping birds around him could be the Shadow Within.

CRACK!

The ear-splitting sound suddenly slashed through the silence and echoed through the clearing. The entire tribe woke up immediately. Cries of alarm and panic filled the air.

A low groan suddenly sounded off in the distance. All heads turned and watched, horrified, as a large branch on the Life Tree began to fall. With a sickening thud, it crashed down onto the branches below. The force of the blow was so powerful that it caused them to snap off the tree. Together, the broken branches plummeted, then collided with the island's jagged ground. Every bird watched, stunned, as some of the branches rolled toward the edge of the island. With a noisy *splash,* the stone-like branches fell into the lake's black waves. Within seconds, they sunk and disappeared from sight, becoming lost to the tribe forever.

Horrible screams exploded around the tribe. Close to Cornelius, a young Healer let out a terrible, dreadful wail. The tribe was in chaos.

A blue jay suddenly flew to the center of the tribe, then hovered in place. His icy eyes darted from blue jay to blue jay as he took in the scene. Atticus let out an ear-splitting cry. It immediately silenced the tribe. All heads turned toward their leader. "Calm yourselves!" Atticus demanded. "If anyone has seen the bird responsible for this treachery, speak now!"

Cornelius felt a twinge of nervousness, his feathers bristling. Should he speak up about his dream? *No,* he decided. *Not while they're in a panic like this. I don't want them thinking that I'm somehow connected to the Shadow Within after sharing a dream with them.*

A bird abruptly shrieked, the noise making Cornelius cringe. Myra and another Protector that Cornelius had never seen before swooped into the clearing. They roughly pecked at a third bird, forcing them forward. When Cornelius realized that it was Alessandra, he let out a gasp.

Myra forced Alessandra to land, then pushed her in front of Atticus. All eyes were on the small blue jay now. Dread pulsed through Cornelius. Atticus was silent for a very long moment as he stared down at the trembling birdess. Then, he landed in front of her. "You?" was all Atticus managed to choke out. "You're the Shadow Within?"

Alessandra's eyes were wide. "No!" she shouted. "It wasn't me, I swear! This is a misunderstanding. Please, you don't understand!"

Myra let out a warning cry, then extended her talons. "Silence!" she hissed. "We spotted you fleeing the Life Tree island right after *you* damaged the tree." She lifted her head, facing her tribemates. "It's clear that Alessandra is the bird responsible for this crime. She must be punished!"

Screams of disgust and rage filled the night. "How could you betray us like this?!" an elder yelled.

Alessandra shook like a small leaf. Her eyes were round and pleading, desperate to make them understand. "You got it all wrong!" Alessandra insisted. "I didn't do this! I would never do this! Please, you have to listen to me. It was someone else. I saw them flying toward the island and I..."

Alessandra trailed off as Atticus took a threatening step toward her. His eyes were bright with anger. "Your lies will not have a place in this tribe any longer," he spat. "You are no longer fit to call yourself a Protector. You will never be one of us again!"

Alessandra's eyes sparkled with tears. To Cornelius' horror, Atticus lifted a talon into the air. He flinched, terrified that the leader would tear the feathers off of the trembling birdess. To his surprise, Atticus only hooked his talon around Alessandra's shoulder and pulled her forward. Atticus lowered his head and told her something in a hushed voice. Alessandra blinked, her eyes growing wide. She took a step backward and stared at Atticus in disbelief.

Atticus grimly waved over Myra and the other Protector. "Take her away," he ordered. Alessandra lowered her head, but didn't object. Countless more Protectors began to swoop down from the trees and landed beside her, wanting to personally escort the Shadow Within out of the tribe.

With one last distraught glance at the tribe, and at Atticus, Alessandra reluctantly unfolded her wings and took off into the night sky. Cornelius watched as she and the swarm of Protectors flew away, becoming small blue specks.

Without warning, a thought slammed into Cornelius, making him gasp. *Alessandra was telling the truth,* he realized with a stinging jolt. *They got the wrong bird!*

# CHAPTER 21

Ellagard gasped as she felt the cold talons of dread coil around her heart. She gazed at the rogue's cave within Misty Falls ruefully. *It's another dream,* she realized. Ellagard let out a groan. *Why does this have to keep happening?*

She knew this dream well. *Since it repeats every single night,* Ellagard wordlessly hissed. But this time, something felt different. Ellagard turned around, expecting to find Khan, her brother, standing in his usual spot during this dream. Ellagard froze. There wasn't a trace of his dark plumage or amber eyes anywhere.

*Strange,* she thought, beginning to feel unnerved. She found the dream to be more unsettling *without* Khan, rather than with him actually being there. *I hate being alone,* Ellagard thought, feeling her plumage bristle. *This is too creepy. Where is he? Khan is always standing there. What caused the dream to change?*

A thought suddenly came to her. "Jarquanzila?" she called out. *When weird stuff starts happening, you can always count on Jarquanzila to be behind it,* Ellagard sarcastically thought. She waited a few seconds for a reply. But, as she had expected, Ellagard had waited in vain, and she got no response.

Ever since Khan had invaded her tribe all of those moons ago, not a single bird reported seeing or hearing from Jarquanzila. It was like he had just... vanished. Ellagard shook her head, pushing the thought away. That didn't matter right now. *I need to focus on this dream,* Ellagard told herself. *No ordinary dream keeps on repeating like this. And now, after countless days, something has changed. I want to know why.*

Suddenly, for the first time, Ellagard noticed the crashing sound of the waterfall, which flowed just outside of the cave. She turned to face it, instantly feeling peaceful as she watched it endlessly fall. Her talons began to tingle, urging her to move closer to the waterfall. Something was calling Ellagard toward it.

Ellagard glanced at the yawning cave on her other side, then peered deep inside of it. All she could see was darkness and emptiness. A chill crawled through Ellagard's plumage, and she shuddered. There was nothing there for Ellagard. She turned her attention back to the waterfall.

With a sigh, she pushed down her fear, lifted her head, and began to walk toward it.

With every step Ellagard took closer to the waterfall, the louder and louder it's rhythmic crashing became. The noise was transfixing, in a way. It filled Ellagard's ears, surrounded her thoughts, and had her complete attention. She forced herself to become detached from it. *It may seem peaceful, but who knows what it really is,* Ellagard thought. *I can't let myself trust it.*

Ellagard was only a feather's length away from the waterfall now. She closed her eyes, expecting to become soaked by its misty spray. She paused, then opened her eyes. Ellagard was right beside the waterfall now, and felt as dry as ever. *Weird,* she thought. Ellagard hesitated for a moment, then gingerly reached out her wing. She placed it under the path of the thundering waterfall.

Ellagard felt nothing.

She folded back her wing, feeling unnerved. Fear crawled beneath her plumage. She didn't like this one bit. *The sooner I stop having these dreams, the better,* Ellagard thought. She looked around, then suddenly felt her blood run cold. A few wing lengths beside Ellagard, right at the edge of the ledge where she stood, rested a heap of boulders. They were stacked, one on top of the other, to create a narrow path. She studied it carefully, then peered upwards.

The path led to the top of Misty Falls.

Ellagard felt her plumage prickle, as if she was being watched. *Something... or someone... wants me to climb the path,* she realized. She did a quick sweep of the dream, finding only the waterfall for company. Ellagard released a heavy sigh. *If I want the dream to stop, I have to do what this bird wants. If they even are a bird.* She shuddered.

Ellagard hesitated for a moment, then began to climb up the steep boulders.

Hours seemed to have passed. Or were they only minutes? Ellagard couldn't be sure. But she did know this: however long she had been trudging up the jagged path, it felt like it had been an eternity. Part of her hoped that she would wake up soon. But another part of her wanted to uncover the mystery behind this dream.

The boulder path coiled around the peak of Misty Falls like a long snake. Ellagard let out a cry of frustration. Would it ever end? Had this been a trap? Would Ellagard ever reach the end, or would she be climbing in vain forever?

She rounded a corner, then let out a gasp. Ellagard could see the last couple of boulders! She was almost at the top of Misty Falls! Ellagard found a sudden burst of energy. She ran forward, determined to finally reach the end. She was just a couple of steps away now!

With a massive leap, Ellagard left the boulders behind. She let out a sigh of relief, then looked around expectantly. A chill slithered through Ellagard's plumage.

The sky above her was grey. But it wasn't from clouds. It was just the colour, plain and empty. Grey seemed to stretch on forever and ever, with no end in sight. In the distance, where the exotic and vibrant jungle should have been, was the eerie grey nothingness as well.

Ellagard felt her heartbeat quicken. She peered over the edge of Misty Falls, then let out a gasp. There was no ground at all! The waterfall seemed to plummet down forever.

Ellagard suddenly felt sick. *I don't want to be in this dream for a moment longer,* she thought.

"Oh really?" said a somber voice. "Why? So you can forget about me for a second time?"

Ellagard's attention snapped toward the direction of the voice. She let out a shaky gasp. "Zander!"

The young peacock's back was turned to her as he stood, unmovingly, on the edge of Misty Falls. He stared blankly into the grey void, his eyes distant and glazed. His turquoise feathers lashed in the wind that Ellagard couldn't feel. As Ellagard saw him, she felt a stab of guilt.

*I forgot about him,* she realized, horrified with herself. Ellagard took a small step toward him. "I'm so sorry, Zander," she murmured. "I'm going to come for you right away. Don't worry. I'll save you soon. I promise."

Zander didn't react. In fact, Ellagard wasn't even sure that her previous trainee had even heard her. "Zander?" she whispered. "A-are you okay?"

Zander slowly turned his head to look at her. His eyes were filled with tears. "You left me here to die," he whispered. His voice broke with the slightest hint of distress. "You never even came back once for me. Did I really mean so little to you? I thought we were friends." His head drooped slightly. "We were friends, weren't we?"

Ellagard felt her heart shatter. "Zander, you meant so much more to me than you'll ever know," she said. "I'm sorry that I left you with the rogues. I... I should have done more to help you. You didn't deserve any of this. Please, forgive me."

Zander's beak curved with the smallest smile. "Thank you, Ellagard," he whispered. "When I see you again, on top of Misty Falls, I hope that you can forgive *me*." And with that, Ellagard's dream began to violently shake.

Ellagard snapped her eyes open, finding herself back in the tribe, in the waking world. "Don't worry, Zander," she whispered, looking up at the moon. "You'll be home soon."

Ellagard lingered awkwardly at the edge of the Protector's sleeping den. Then, she ducked her head and stepped inside. Ellagard almost immediately tripped over the lump of feathers that was her brother, Cyprus. Ellagard, forcing back a groan of annoyance, scanned the den for Reyna. *She's the only bird I trust to know my plan,* she thought. If news broke out that the tribe's leader was heading straight into rogue territory by herself, the tribe would become plunged into chaos. *No one other than Reyna can know.*

Eventually, Ellagard spotted her. Anger surged through her. *Of course Reyna's sleeping at the very back of the den,* Ellagard sarcastically thought. *Why wouldn't she be in the most difficult spot to get to, especially when I'm in a hurry?* Ellagard forced herself to smooth down her plumage. Being frustrated wouldn't help anything right now.

Ellagard scanned the mass of sleeping peacocks. It would be impossible to slip past them all without waking someone up. Annoyance began to bubble in her chest. This was urgent, and Ellagard was wasting time! "Reyna!" Ellagard called in a loud whisper.

The sleeping birdess didn't react. In her frustration, Ellagard went to dig her talons into the earth underfoot. Sharp pain abruptly rushed up her leg. She looked down, and saw that she had accidentally sunk her talons into a small twig. Ellagard was sure that she had more than one splinter in her foot now, but she didn't care.

This was an opportunity.

Ellagard picked the twig up with her beak, then flung it (a little bit harder than she had meant to) at Reyna. It hit her in the forehead with a pitiful *thunk*. She woke up immediately, confusion and annoyance glittering in her yellow eyes. Rubbing her forehead with her wing, Reyna picked up the twig in her talons and studied it angrily. Then, she spotted Ellagard. "What was that for?" she whispered.

Ellagard signaled for her to follow with a wing, then left the den to wait for her. After a few moments, Reyna slid outside, looking sleepy. "What's wrong?" she asked with a huge yawn, once they were out of earshot of their tribemates.

Ellagard quickly told Reyna everything. How Zander had survived, how Khan and his rogues were keeping him at Misty Falls, and how Ellagard was about to go and rescue him.

Once Ellagard was finished, Reyna blinked, looking surprised. "So you're leaving, just like that?" she asked in disbelief. Ellagard nodded. Reyna's eyes flashed with concern. "But that's crazy! You can't leave. You have a tribe to lead."

Ellagard rolled her eyes. "I *know*," she said, feeling annoyed. She was wasting time. "But I've already made up my mind. I'm going."

Reyna let out a disdainful sniff. "So what are you going to do? Waltz right up into rogue territory and expect to leave there alive?" Her white feather's bristled. "Yeah, good luck with that."

Ellagard was impatient now. "That's exactly what I'm going to do, if it's quite alright with you," she retorted, pushing past Reyna. "Just watch the camp for me while I'm gone. I'll be back soon with Zander." *I hope...* she thought.

Reyna ran forward until she walked side-by-side with Ellagard. "I'm not letting you go by yourself," she insisted.

"Yes, you are," Ellagard responded, trying to keep her voice steady. She was beginning to regret telling Reyna about her plan to rescue

Zander. "Stay here and watch the camp. The tribe needs you to be here while I'm gone."

Before Reyna had a chance to object, Ellagard picked up speed and left her deputy behind. This was something that Ellagard needed to do alone. *I'm not going to lose another bird that I love,* Ellagard thought. *Zander was my responsibility, and now I'm going to make things right.*

As Ellagard ran into the untamed jungle beyond the camp, she felt determination flow through her veins. *Don't worry Zander. I'm coming.*

# CHAPTER 22

Cornelius gripped the branch tighter. *They got the wrong bird!* He felt fear flash through him as he recalled his shared dream with the Shadow Within. Cornelius remembered the colour of their plumage. *It had been a dark blue,* he thought. Then, Cornelius lifted his head. He peered beyond the camp, past the lake, and then at the swarm of Protectors flying in the distance. He spotted Alessandra instantly. It was easy to pick her out from the rest.

Alessandra's pale, sky-blue feathers were striking against the dark, inky sky. Cornelius felt a flash of fear. *The colour of their feathers don't match. Alessandra isn't a Shadow Within,* he thought. *So that means that they're still in the camp somewhere!* As Cornelius warily looked around, he realized that most of the tribe had dark blue feathers. It would be next to impossible to figure out the Shadow Within's identity, just based off of the colour of their plumage alone.

*I'm so sorry, Alessandra,* Cornelius wordlessly told her, watching as she and the swarm of Protectors disappeared with distance. *I promise that I'll find the true traitor soon.*

By now, the night sky was slowly beginning to fill with light. It was the start of a new day. And that meant that it was another day closer to the moon becoming full. Cornelius shuddered, remembering what the Shadow Within had told him in the dream. *When the moon becomes full, they will become the most powerful bird in the world,* he remembered.

Cornelius sighed. He cringed, realizing how loud the sound had been. For the first time, he noticed how silent the tribe was. Not a single bird spoke. Not a single bird moved. Not a single bird celebrated what they thought was the removal of the Shadow Within. Cornelius felt the somber mood wash over him, and he quickly realized why the tribe was so grim. *They still think of Alessandra as a beloved tribemate,* he thought in surprise. *Even despite what they think she's done.*

Cornelius hung his head, taking the time to think. That was all he could do for now. Cornelius had made a huge discovery about the Shadow Within, but yet he felt as lost as ever. *All I know about them is the colour of their plumage, and that I'll be powerless to stop them in a couple more days,* he thought, feeling grim. *That information doesn't help me in the slightest.*

The tribe's silence was broken by the sound of many flapping wings. Commander Myra and the other Protectors had returned. They too looked grim.

All except for Myra.

Cornelius watched her, feeling anger spark through his plumage. She looked pleased with herself. Cornelius clenched his beak. Then, he noticed the colour of her plumage. *It's dark blue,* he thought. Cornelius hadn't forgotten how Myra had set them up with the patrol all those days ago, when they had met with the seagulls. *It's like she* knew *that we would run into them,* Cornelius thought darkly.

Cornelius' eyes became hooded as he thought. *Myra also seemed so quick to keep Alessandra silent,* he remembered. *She wouldn't let her speak, and instead accused her every chance she could. Why would Myra do this, if she didn't want to keep something hidden?* Cornelius sunk his talons deeper into the bark. Suddenly, the branch he stood on creaked slightly.

Instinctively, Cornelius whirled around and extended his talons, feeling his heartbeat quicken. He relaxed when he spotted Shadow. She looked at her friend, concern glittering in her eyes. Just before Shadow could question Cornelius' jumpy behaviour, Dustin came and landed close beside his fellow SkyTalons. His dark blue feathers were fluffed out against the chilly morning breeze.

Cornelius blinked at his friends questioningly, not daring to speak. He didn't want to disturb the silent, grieving tribe. And by the looks of it, Shadow and Dustin didn't want to, either.

Shadow pointed at the sky with her wing. Then, she swooped into the cold air, leading the way out of the tribe.


The SkyTalons had only flown a small distance outside of the camp. They landed on a sturdy pine tree, certain that they were now out of earshot of the tribe.

The moment Shadow folded her wings back, she looked at Cornelius nervously. "I can tell that something's troubling you," she told him. "What's wrong?"

Cornelius quickly told them everything. About his shared dream with the Shadow Within, his suspicions about Myra, and how he knew that Alessandra was innocent. "Her feathers are pale blue," Cornelius explained. "And the shadow's feathers were a dark blue. There's no way that Alessandra is the traitor."

Dustin frowned, considering Cornelius' words. "But, didn't you say that there was more than one Shadow Within?" he asked. "Alessandra could still be a traitor. Just not the one you saw in your dream."

Shadow nodded. "Dustin brings up a good point," she said. "And it *is* strange that Alessandra was interested in the tree. Even if she is innocent, why was she watching it so closely, to the point that she noticed some bird fly over to the island? It just seems odd to me." Shadow's gaze darkened with thought. "While I'm not sure if Alessandra really is a traitor, there is one bird that I have great suspicions with."

Dustin froze, looking at Shadow expectantly. Cornelius blinked. "Who?" he asked.

Shadow stood taller. "Myra," she told them. "Since the day we first arrived here, I've always gotten a bad vibe from her. There's just something off with Myra, and I can't explain it. But whatever it is, I don't like it one bit."

Cornelius nodded, letting out a sigh of relief. He was glad that some bird agreed with him. "I feel like she purposely set us up with that patrol the other day," he confessed. "It was like she just knew that we would run into danger, and put us in a patrol that wouldn't be as strong in a fight."

Dustin sat silently, taking in Cornelius' and Shadow's words. The two SkyTalons turned to look at him.

"What do you think, Dustin?" Shadow asked. "You've lived in this tribe longer than we have. If anyone has a good sense of who the Shadow Within really is, it's going to be you."

Dustin shook his head. "I'm sorry," he said, "but your guess is as good as mine." The blue jay suddenly looked angry. "If you want my honest opinion though, I still think that Atticus is a Shadow Within. I know that you two are starting to trust him, even if you won't admit it. But if I were you, I would watch my back around him."

Shadow and Cornelius were silent for a moment, unsure of how to respond to Dustin's grim words. Then, Shadow spoke after carefully thinking about her next words. "It doesn't matter *who* the Shadow Within is. At least not at the moment," she began. "What we need now is a plan. Whoever these birds are, they seem to have one solid motive. They won't stop until they destroy the Life Tree. Because if they do, every tribe will fall, and we'll lose everything."

Cornelius nodded. "We can't let that happen," he added. "I say that we guard the tree so that they can't damage it any further. And we'll bide our time until the full moon arrives. Hopefully by then, we'd have uncovered their identity, and have put a stop to their plans, once and for all."

Without warning, the leaves overhead began to shake. Cornelius felt a flash of fear. He jumped to his talons and moved in closer to Shadow and Dustin, ready to fight to protect them. After a few moments, the scrawny shape of Atticus appeared. The leader swooped down and landed beside the three SkyTalons.

Something dark appeared in Dustin's eyes as he gazed at his father. The small blue jay slowly slid his talons deep into the bark underfoot.

Atticus' frosty gaze slithered past each SkyTalon in turn. He lingered for an extra second longer on Dustin, his expression unreadable. Then, finally, he looked away, instead turning his attention back to Shadow and Cornelius.

"I agree with your plan," Atticus told them. "And I am prepared to do whatever it takes to stop the true Shadows Within."

# CHAPTER 23

Shadow and Cornelius exchanged a glance. *Atticus wants to help us?* Cornelius thought, surprised. He never would have guessed that the secretive, cold leader would be willing to work with the SkyTalons on *anything*, let alone finding and stopping the Shadows Within.

*But it makes sense,* Cornelius realized. *He may not like us in the slightest, but he truly does care about his tribe. If he's willing to put aside his differences with us, then we should be willing to do the same. And besides, if we're going to stop the Shadows Within before the full moon arrives, we're going to need all the help we can get.*

But Dustin clearly didn't feel the same way. Anger burned in his blue eyes, and his feathers were slowly beginning to flare. "No," Dustin snarled at Atticus. "We want nothing to do with you. And why were you following us, anyways?"

Atticus looked at his son nonchalantly. "I'm the leader of this tribe," he began. "I notice when birds abruptly leave the camp, and it's my job to find out why."

Atticus suddenly looked angry. "And I would watch my *tone* if I were you," he growled. "Don't think that just because you're a SkyTalon now means that you can go around doing anything you please."

For the briefest of moments, fear flashed across Dustin's face. But that moment didn't last long, and the cold glint in Dustin's eyes returned. Father and son locked gazes for a tense moment, and silence gripped the forest.

Shadow quickly stepped in between the two blue jays, looking worried. "We mustn't fight," she told them. Then, Shadow met Atticus' gaze. "We would be grateful for your help. These are difficult times for everyone. The more birds we have working together to stop the Shadows Within, the more likely we will succeed."

Dustin let out a huff of disbelief. "Did you not hear a single thing I said earlier?" he demanded, looking at Cornelius and Shadow. Then, he turned his furious gaze onto Atticus. "He can't be trusted," Dustin spat, looking straight into his father's pale eyes.

Dustin broke his gaze away after a few seconds, whipping around to face his fellow SkyTalons.

"In fact, I think that our *traitor* might be standing right in front of us!" Dustin yelled, starting to lose control of his temper. The more he spoke, the more fury slipped into his voice. "It wouldn't be the first time he betrayed innocent birds! Isn't that right, *father*?"

Atticus was silent for a very long time as he stared at his son, his expression unreadable. "Whatever," he murmured at last, "I'm not going through this again." Atticus turned to look at Shadow and Cornelius, flicking Dustin in the beak with his tail feathers as he did so. "Let's have a serious discussion about the Shadows Within, shall we?" he told them.

Cornelius shifted uneasily. He found it strange to have a peaceful, and for the most part, calm, encounter with the tribe's leader. *Atticus looks a lot less villainous, now that I know he's not a Shadow Within,* Cornelius realized. Atticus looked stressed, more than anything. His eyes were hooded from his lack of sleep, and his feathers were unkempt, as if he didn't have the time to groom them.

"I think that we should have at least one bird on the island, guarding the Life Tree at all times," Atticus began, lifting his head. "The three of us will take turns, so that way we'll..." he trailed off when he spotted Dustin.

The small blue jay was digging his talons so fiercely into the branch underfoot that it began to splinter. "What do you mean, the *three* of us?" Dustin softly growled. "Are you not including me in this plan?" There was a threat in his voice.

"Oh yes, that reminds me," Atticus began, turning to look at Dustin. "As leader of the tribe, I forbid you from ever setting foot on the Life Tree island again. If a bird catches you so much as glancing at the tree, they have my permission to banish you forever."

"What!?" Dustin screamed, outraged.

Cornelius' orange eyes grew wide. *But Dustin is the tribe's Speaker,* he thought, horrified. *Atticus can't just ban him from going to the Life Tree... can he?*

"I'm a SkyTalon now," Dustin dangerously growled. Something in his eyes seemed to have snapped. "So that means that I'm above every bird in every tribe, including you. If I want to go to the Life Tree island, I can. Do you *really* think that any bird is going to *dare* stand in my way?"

Cornelius looked at Dustin nervously. *That doesn't seem like something Dustin would ever say,* he thought. *What happened to that kind, shy, and awkward bird that I first met inside of Jajarii? He seems just so... bitter... now.*

Shadow seemed to have noticed this as well. "Dustin, stand down," she said. "I know you may not like it, but Atticus isn't just your father. He's the tribe's leader, too. You have to do what he says."

Dustin's eyes became hooded with shadows. He dug his talons in and out of the bark below, his beak clenching. "Fine," he spat. "If you're going to keep me from the Life Tree, then I'll just go and find the real Shadow Within myself. And then you'll just see how wrong you were about me."

With a final seething look at Shadow, Atticus, and Cornelius, Dustin unfolded his wings and flew off. Within moments, the blue jay disappeared into the dense forest, leaving the others in a grim silence.

Atticus was the first to speak. "I know that you may think badly of me," he began. "But believe it or not, I'm only doing what's best for the tribe... and for Dustin. I know my son better than anyone. Everything I've done, no matter how terrible it may seem at first, has been for good reasons."

Shadow narrowed her eyes, her scar glinting in the murky light. "As much as I disagree with some of your decisions, I still honour them," she began. "You are the leader of the tribe, and were a SkyTalon before us." Shadow let out a sigh. "But if I'm being honest, I don't think that I would have agreed with your plan to help us if you weren't either of those things. You may have your reasons, but I find that you're cold and heartless around your son."

Shadow worriedly looked in the direction where Dustin flew off, concerned for his safety. Her wingtips twitched slightly in her eagerness to catch up with the young blue jay. But Shadow forced herself to remain still, and to hear the rest of Atticus' plan.

Atticus looked away from her. "My family issues don't matter right now," he told them. "Right now, we need to come up with a plan. Soon, the moon will be full, and if we don't stop the Shadows Within before then, we will lose *everything*."

Cornelius shook his head. "We won't let that happen," he said. Then, he stood taller. "Let's figure out how we can save the tribe. We're going to stop the Shadows Within, once and for all. And, we're going to do it together."

# CHAPTER 24

The Life Tree island was still in the night. Not even the waves from the lake dared to crash against the shore.

It was Cornelius' turn to guard the Life Tree for the night. Atticus, Shadow, and him had all agreed to the plan: each night, until daybreak, the three of them would take turns to guard the tree.

The moon shone brightly onto the island below, bathing it and the Life Tree in its silver light. As Cornelius gazed up at the moon, he began to feel a twinge of unease. *It's almost full,* he thought, nervous. *Soon, maybe in just a night or two, it'll be whole. And then the Shadow Within will be at their full power, and we'll have lost everything.*

Cornelius felt a shiver crawl down his spine. He refused to let that happen! He would fight with all the strength he had to stop the Shadows Within. *No matter what happens to me, I will make sure that the tribes survive,* he told himself.

Cornelius suddenly felt a stab of bitterness. "Are you happy now, grandfather?" he muttered under his breath, as if Donovan was actually there. "I'm doing everything you wanted. Maybe even more."

Cornelius slowly extended his talons. "While I'm here in the tribe risking *my* life every night to fix your mistakes, you're living comfortably back in the city. You have everything that I don't. My family. My friends. My home." Cornelius hung his head, feeling the sting of betrayal. "You used me, grandfather," he whimpered.

Before he could stop himself, tears began to flow from his eyes. "I trusted you so much. I respected you. I loved you. And I thought that you felt the same way. But I was clearly wrong," Cornelius continued. "You knew deep down that I was going to end up being a SkyTalon one day. That's why you acted like you cared about me. Just so you could eventually send me away, so I could fix your mistakes."

Cornelius sunk deeper into his plumage. "Would you even care if I never came back?" he asked, imagining the blue and green eyes of his grandfather. *Would they have filled with sorrow at this question?* Cornelius wondered. A tear streaked down his face. "Would it even matter to you?" Cornelius continued, his voice breaking. "You only ever saw me as something disposable. And you might never even get a chance to try and deny it."

Cornelius turned to gaze at the Life Tree. "In a night or two, the Shadow Within is going to become unstoppable, if we don't defeat them before then. I might get injured or worse, and never see my flock and home again. And it'll be because of you." Cornelius felt his heart shatter. He was beginning to feel overwhelmed.

Cornelius forced himself to push away his horrible feelings. *I can't let myself get distracted,* he told himself. *What's done is done. If Donovan really cares so little about me, I can't do anything to change that. But I can change the fate of the tribes. It's up to me, Shadow, Atticus, and Dustin to save the Life Tree.*

Cornelius lifted his head, extended his talons, and began to protectively circle the island. As he did so, he occasionally shot suspicious looks at the camp in the distance. He half expected

Commander Myra to come slinking out of the shadows, ready to attack him and the Life Tree at any moment. Cornelius still couldn't shake the feeling that she was indeed a Shadow Within. *I wouldn't trust her with a single one of my feathers,* Cornelius thought, coming to a halt.

Cornelius remembered Atticus' words, after Shadow and him had told the leader about their suspicions with Myra. "No," Atticus had bluntly said. "Commander Myra is a strong, level-headed bird. I chose her to lead the Protectors myself. I've known her since she was a hatchling. She is loyal to me, and to her tribe. And while she may be a bit too proud, Myra would never betray us."

Atticus had shot a teasing look at Shadow and Cornelius. "Since she has such a high status in the tribe, Myra feels threatened by having to compete with the three *almighty* and *legendary* SkyTalons," he had said. "Obviously, she's afraid that you three are overshadowing her. That's why she isn't grovelling at your talons like the rest of the tribe is. *Don't* mistake that as treason."

Now, Cornelius felt himself droop like a withering plant. *Is it wrong that I kind of believe Atticus?* he asked himself. *He trusts Myra so much. And now I'm finding myself trusting Atticus...* Cornelius buried his head in his wings. He felt so confused.

*So, let's just say that Myra isn't a Shadow Within after all. Then who is?* he wondered. *No bird fits the role of a traitor like Myra does. And we've only met a talonful of birds in this tribe. This Shadow Within could be anyone.* Cornelius frowned, thinking carefully. *Let's see... there's Nathaniel. But, he's so shy and cautious. I think he's scared of his own shadow. He can't be the traitor. Then there's Alessandra. She seems nothing but kind. I don't think Alessandra would want to harm anyone. And she looked so terrified, right before she had been banished. No traitor could act that innocent.* He felt a flash of guilt, knowing that she was out there right now, all alone. Cornelius wordlessly promised himself that he would find her soon, and bring her back to the tribe.

*And then finally, there's Dustin. But that's just ridiculous to even think about. Dustin is a SkyTalon, and my friend. He would never betray the tribes.* Cornelius let out a sigh. *So then, who would?* he pondered.

Cornelius began to pace, his talons clicking against the stone ground underfoot. *Who could possibly be a Shadow Within?* he asked himself. *Who could have managed to slip by after all this time, completely undetected? Who could have been so cunning that not even a single bird suspected them? Who could have managed to do all of* this *damage?* Cornelius came to a halt in front of one of the broken branches of the Life Tree, looking at it remorsefully.

As Cornelius continued to circle the island once more, the air around him began to feel thinner and thinner. The remaining branches on the Life Tree seemed to loom in on him. His plumage felt like heavy boulders. Cornelius' heart began to race, and he quickly glanced up at the moon. *I'm running out of time,* he told himself. Only a sliver of the moon remained hidden. *I don't have any proof that Myra really is the Shadow Within. It might not even be her in the first place.* He felt his heart beat faster. And faster. And even faster. *What am I going to do if I can't discover their identity on time? All of the tribes will fall, and it'll be all my fault.*

The sound of flapping wings suddenly emerged from the silence, making Cornelius jump. He extended his talons and whirled around to face the direction of the noise.

Cornelius let out a sigh of relief when he spotted the fluffy shape of Shadow gliding toward him. When he saw her, all of Cornelius' worries melted away. With Shadow by his side, Cornelius knew that everything would be fine.

"Hi," Cornelius said when she came to land beside him. The small pigeon felt warm from talons to beak when Shadow smiled at him.

"Hello, Cornelius," Shadow replied. She looked at him teasingly. "I'm sure you've had a blast."

Cornelius laughed. "Oh, I had the time of my life!" he jokingly exclaimed. "I'm sure you'll have just as much fun as I had. There are plenty of pebbles to keep you company, if you get bored. But there's no chance that'll happen."

Shadow giggled.

Cornelius smiled. He loved seeing Shadow, the bird he loved so much, happy. *If she's happy, then I'm happy.*

After Shadow stopped laughing, she looked into Cornelius' eyes. "Go get some rest," she told him, "you've earned it. I'll continue to watch the Life Tree until it's Atticus' turn."

Cornelius looked at her gratefully. He unfolded his wings and swooped into the inky night sky. As he flew over the lake and into the camp, he made sure to fly as silently as possible, not wanting to wake any of the sleeping blue jays.

Cornelius spotted Dustin amongst the crowd. His friend looked tense, even in sleep. Dustin's blue feathers were ruffled slightly, and his talons were tightly clamped around the branch he slept on. Cornelius felt a flash of pity for his friend. *Dustin must be having a nightmare,* he realized, wishing there was something he could do for his fellow SkyTalon.

Cornelius' mind suddenly flew back in time, to when he had been a hatchling. *Whenever I was having a bad dream, I was strangely comforted in the middle of it, and the nightmare would just disappear,* he remembered. *When I would wake up in the morning, I would always find grandfather close to my side, giving me warmth and protection.*

Cornelius felt a twinge of sadness, grimly realizing how that had been nothing but manipulation, so that he would grow up trusting Donovan.

*While grandfather's love may have been a lie, I truly care about Dustin,* he told himself. Cornelius glided over to his sleeping friend, then landed carefully beside him. *Maybe that's all Dustin needs right now. A bird by his side who cares about him.* Cornelius sunk deeper into his feathers, closed his eyes, then felt the peace of sleep wash over him.

*Don't worry Dustin,* he sleepily thought. *I have a feeling that everything is going to be okay.*

# CHAPTER 25

Cornelius looked around, feeling the biggest smile grow on his face. Could it really be possible? He listened to the vrooming of cars, and the chattering of the countless no-feathers down below. Cornelius drew in a deep breath, feeling joy rush through his feathers.

He was here! He was home! Cornelius was back in the city! He let out an excited laugh, looking around eagerly. Part of him had thought that he would never see his home again. But now, here he was! And the city was as perfect as he remembered it to be. Oh, how he missed it here!

Cornelius was high up in the sky, standing on the flat roof of one of the many gigantic no-feather towers. He briskly walked over to the edge and peered down below. He let out a gasp of awe. Cornelius' home was beautiful.

Suddenly, a thought struck him. If Cornelius was back in his city home, then that must mean...

"Cornelius?" a soft voice called from behind him. Cornelius turned around, then let out a gasp of sheer joy. All around him was his flock. His friends and family!

Before he could help it, happy tears escaped from Cornelius' big orange eyes. Emotions flooded through him.

Cornelius spotted his siblings, Jemma and Xavier, and immediately rushed over to greet them. They both had wide, perfect, identical smiles on their faces. Even Xavier looked more cheerful than normal. It was just how Cornelius always wanted him to be... happy.

Cornelius wrapped his wings around Jemma first, and then Xavier. His siblings continued to smile at him.

Suddenly, Cornelius' flock began to shift, and the tall shape of Donovan stepped forward. He too had a massive smile on his face. "Hello, grandson of mine!" he exclaimed happily, the smile not once wavering. "Oh, how pleased we all are to see you again. We missed you, Cornelius."

All at once, Cornelius' flock gathered around him. They embraced him in their many wings.

"Welcome back, Cornelius."

"We missed you, Cornelius."

"Good to see you again, Cornelius."

Cornelius let himself melt away in their wings, feeling his heart soar with his endless love for his flock. He had missed them so much. And, for the longest time, Cornelius had thought that they didn't feel the same way. *I never thought that I would be so happy to be proven wrong,* Cornelius thought.

The flock all stepped back at the same time.

Donovan looked at his grandson warmly, still smiling. "We are so proud of you, Cornelius," he told him. Donovan slowly unfolded a wing, then placed it on Cornelius' shoulder. The elderly pigeon happily continued on. "And now that you have finally completed your SkyTalon work, you can stay home, where you belong."

Cornelius paused, feeling a twinge of unease. Was he ready to leave Shadow, the bird he loved so much, behind? And what about

Dustin, his best friend? Cornelius was surprised by just how much he had grown to care for the tribes as well.

"Thank you, grandfather," he began, "But I just can't come home yet. I'm not ready to leave my new life behind. I know that I've completed all my missions as a SkyTalon, but I just can't help feeling like there is something... big... happening soon."

Donovan smiled, still keeping his wing on Cornelius' shoulder.

Cornelius blinked, feeling confused. He touched a talon to his forehead. "What *was* supposed to happen soon?" he wondered out loud. "I remember that it was something terrible. And that the moon was involved somehow. But why...?"

Donovan tightened his wing's grip on Cornelius' shoulder ever so slightly, continuing to smile. "We are so proud of you, Cornelius," Donovan repeated. "And now that you have finally completed your SkyTalon work, you can stay home, where you belong."

Cornelius brushed off his grandfather's wing, then took a few steps back. "But I still have to fix something," he breathed, starting to feel nervous. He closed his eyes, thinking carefully. *I can't remember what it was,* he realized. *Didn't some other bird have something happen to them, just like this? Wasn't her name... Alexandra. No, that isn't it. Wasn't it Alessandra? Yes, I think that's it. She couldn't remember something important. I can't remember something important. Why do I have a feeling that this is more than a coincidence?*

When Cornelius opened his eyes again, he jumped, recoiling from surprise.

Jemma and Xavier had appeared in front of him, looking as gleeful as ever. "This is where you belong, Cornelius," they both said in unison, sending a chill down his spine. "Here, with us. Your flock. Not the tribes."

Cornelius began to feel uncomfortable. Every smiling face was watching him... unblinkingly. He gulped, taking another step backward. "I'm so sorry," he told them all. "But I just can't join you. Not yet. Please understand."

Another pigeon stepped forward, standing side-by-side with Jemma and Xavier. Her warm, round amber eyes looked at Cornelius happily. Cornelius felt a flash of guilt the moment he saw her. *It's Corra,* he realized, feeling a strange hole open up in his heart. *The pigeon who I had loved before I even knew what a SkyTalon was. But there's another bird that I love now... Shadow.* "I'm sorry," Cornelius whispered to her, unsure of why he felt so guilty. He almost felt as though he had betrayed her in some way. "You were one of the most amazing birds I knew."

Corra continued to smile, looking unphased. "You belong here," she insisted, "with me. With us."

William, Jemma's mate, stepped forward. "You belong here, Cornelius," he said. Cornelius briskly nodded. He was desperate to make them understand.

"You belong here."

"This is your home."

"The city is where you're meant to be."

"You belong here, you belong here, you belong here, you..."

Cornelius covered his ears with his wings as the whole flock chanted those words in unison, over and over again. He crumpled to the ground, feeling his heart fiercely pound. All of his inner conflicts on where he truly belonged in this world began to clash inside of him, making him feel dizzy. *I'm a pigeon, so I can never truly be a part of the tribes,* he realized. *But I'm also a SkyTalon, so I can never truly be a part of the city.*

"You belong here, you belong here, you belong..."

"Stop it!" Cornelius shouted. "Stop, please! I belong with the tribes now! I'm so sorry." Cornelius looked around, expecting a collection of hurt and wounded faces on his flockmates.

Instead, they continued to smile at him.

Donovan, his eyes warm with joy, lowered his head slightly so that he matched Cornelius' height. "Then if you don't belong with us, you belong nowhere in this world," he said through his perfect smile.

Cornelius flinched, as if he had been struck by merciless talons. Without warning, memories began to come flooding back to him. Cornelius remembered how Donovan had used him, manipulating him to become a SkyTalon in his absence. Cornelius remembered what his mission was. Cornelius remembered what he still had to do. *I need to stop the Shadows Within,* he told himself.

Cornelius felt a gasp escape from his beak. *Grandfather may have manipulated me, but he was never cruel to me,* he thought. *None of this is real. This is all a dream!* Cornelius never could have formed a dream so vivid, so clear, on his own. So that means that some other bird must have!

Cornelius gazed past his joyful flockmates and at the city beyond. He hurriedly scanned the many rooftops around him. Then, Cornelius felt his breath get caught in his throat.

It was a blue jay!

Cornelius peered at them carefully, desperate to make out their identity. But they were too far away to be sure. The blue jay stood on the next building over, and was covered by a hazy, white fog that filled Cornelius' dream. It masked their face.

The blue jay gently tapped their talon on the cement roof, and Xavier immediately lifted his head. Cornelius' attention was pulled toward his imposter brother. "You never really did belong here anyways, Cornelius," Xavier stated.

As he spoke, Cornelius turned his head to look at the blue jay. Their beak was moving in unison with Xavier's words. *It's not my flockmates speaking at all,* Cornelius realized, terrified. *It's the Shadow Within controlling them!*

"You were always just in my way, Cornelius," Jemma, or the Shadow Within, said.

Donovan moved in closer. "I tried to warn you. I tried to save you. But now you will be destroyed, alongside my pathetic tribemates," they hissed.

Without warning, within the blink of an eye, every one of Cornelius' imposter flockmates vanished, leaving him all alone on the rooftop. Cornelius whipped around and watched, feeling his heart skip a beat, as the blue jay began to walk away. They gave Cornelius a final bored look before lifting a wing high up into the air. Then, they roughly slammed it against the concrete floor.

The dream began to rumble. The dream began to melt away. The dream began to become filled with shadows!

"No!' Cornelius screamed. This had all been a trap! Within seconds, the entire city had been replaced with black, liquidly shadows. With a sickening squelch, Cornelius' talons were pulled under. He desperately tried to dislodge the gooey shadows, but it was no use.

Cornelius was stuck.

He quickly flung open his wings and flapped as hard as he could. Slowly, the shadows began to slither up his feathers. They coiled around Cornelius' wings, weighing them down. Fear exploded through him. He couldn't fly.

Cornelius watched, helpless, as the blue jay lifted up a talon into the air. They slowly made a scratching motion, just like Jarquanzila had done in Jajarii so long ago. Within seconds, a rift appeared. Cornelius felt a rush of terror. On the other side was another world... another dream. *It's theirs*, Cornelius realized, feeling a spike of horror. *The Shadow Within is escaping!*

Cornelius gritted his beak. He wasn't going to let them flee so easily! This could be his last chance to discover who they really were, before the full moon arrived.

"So long, Cornelius!" the blue jay called over. "I wish fate didn't have to make us enemies. But I will not leave a single bird who stands in my way alive." Then, without a moment's hesitation, the blue jay leapt into the rift, and into their own dream.

They were now safe on the other side.

And Cornelius was all alone, fighting for his life.

The cold, terrible shadows continued to creep up Cornelius' plumage. They were going to suffocate him, if he didn't escape soon. Every second that passed, the deeper Cornelius was pulled into the gooey, black liquid. Panic began to explode through him. His breath came in sharp wheezes. *I'm going to die,* he realized.

Cornelius began to think of Shadow, and tears fell from his eyes. *I never even confessed my feelings to her,* he thought. *She'll never know that I love her. And once I'm gone, she'll be all alone.* A sob gripped him. *And so will Dustin. What will happen to the two of them without me? Will they just be replaced as SkyTalons, like Atticus and Ellagard were when Donovan left them?* Cornelius felt his shoulders sag as the heavy shadows collected on top of him. *And what about the tribes? The Shadows Within will destroy every single one of them.*

Cornelius suddenly felt a rush of determination. *There are innocent birds in each tribe,* he told himself. *They don't deserve what the Shadow Within has planned for them.* Cornelius felt himself get pulled under even further. *What am I doing? I need to fight! I can't give up. If I do, I'm giving up on all of those innocent lives.*

The shadows were up to Cornelius' chest now. He was sinking fast. "Come on, Cornelius," he told himself. With all of his might, he managed to pull one of his wings free from the grip of the shadows. Then, with a gritted beak, he managed to break his other wing free. Exhaustion began to swamp Cornelius. His talons were still stuck.

But he refused to give up!

Cornelius lowered his head and clamped his beak around the shadows covering his talons. Then, he began to tug. And tugged some more. And tugged with all of his might. But it was no use. The soppy shadows didn't budge. Cornelius let out a cry of frustration. *Come on,* he urged himself, *I can do this.*

Cornelius extended his wings and began to flap as hard as he could. After a few seconds, his wings began to burn. But Cornelius continued on.

He had to flap harder. He had to break free. He had to see Shadow and Dustin again. He had to save the tribes!

With a final fierce flap of his wings, Cornelius' talons were released with a loud squelch. Cornelius felt himself lift up into the air. He was free! Cornelius let out a sigh of relief, then looked around. Throughout the void of squirming, oozing, pulsing shadows, Cornelius spotted the rift that the blue jay had used to escape from his dream. Then, he let out a terrified gasp.

The rift was beginning to seal itself. In a few more moments, it would close, and Cornelius would be trapped inside of this nightmare forever. "Never!" he screamed, feeling adrenaline tear through his veins. Cornelius exploded forward. He flapped his wings harder. He felt the wind whip past his feathers. He felt his eyes water.

The inky shadows rose up in spikes as he flew, blocking his path. Cornelius narrowed his eyes, then swerved to the side, avoiding them. He refused to let anything slow him down. No matter what the void and the Shadow Within threw at him, Cornelius would be ready. He *must* reach the rift in time. It became smaller and smaller with every flap of Cornelius' wings.

He forced himself to fly even faster than ever before. The world around him exploded past in a blur. More and more shadows rose up, blocking him. Cornelius avoided them by only a feather's length.

Time was running out. The rift would close in about five more seconds. Cornelius flew even faster.

Four more seconds. Cornelius accidentally hit his wing against one of the shadows, but continued on as surely as ever, despite the pain.

Three more seconds.

The rift was only a sliver now.

Two more seconds.

Another shadow exploded upwards. Cornelius narrowly avoided colliding into it.

One more second.

With all of the strength Cornelius had left, he forced himself to explode forward in a flash. He slammed his eyes shut, protecting them from the slashing wind. A strange warmth slid over Cornelius' feathers. The rift had sealed itself closed.

Cornelius blinked open his eyes, feeling dizzy. Then, he let out a sigh of relief. By some miracle, Cornelius had made it to the other side. He was safe... or as safe as he could be inside of the Shadow Within's dream. Then, Cornelius felt his blood turn into ice.

Horror, dread, and disbelief slashed his heart with talons as sharp as thorns. The world around Cornelius blurred, and he felt his wings give out on him. He fell, hitting the floor with a thump. The ground

began to sway from under him. "No," Cornelius whispered. "No, no, no."
Cornelius found himself face-to-face with the Shadow Within. Cornelius found himself face-to-face with the blue jay.

Cornelius found himself face-to-face with Dustin.

# CHAPTER 26

Cornelius felt his breath snag in his throat, then snag again as he gasped with disbelief. He looked at Dustin... at the Shadow Within... and felt dread surge through him.

"Please," Cornelius whimpered, dragging himself to his talons. "Please tell me that you're not one of them. Please tell me that you're not a Shadow Within."

Dustin was silent for a very long moment, looking grim. His eyes were dark, perfectly mirroring his dream, as he stared at Cornelius. "I'm sorry it had to come to this," Dustin stated flatly. Then, he slowly extended his talons. "But I'm not letting anyone get in my way. Not even you, Cornelius."

Cornelius looked at Dustin weakly, starting to feel dizzy. He staggered on his talons slightly. The cold, ruthless talons of betrayal stabbed into Cornelius' heart. How could his friend have done this to the tribes... to him? *Dustin fooled us all,* he realized, wishing that he could bury his head in his wings. *All those times the Life Tree was damaged, all those times where innocent lives were in danger... it was him. Dustin was behind all of it.*

Dustin's dream was empty, looking just like the void of Jajarii. Blackness seemed to stretch on forever and ever. The only thing that could be seen was a huge, full moon that hung just a couple of wing lengths above the two SkyTalon's heads. Its murky, pale light swamped down onto them. Dustin looked eerie in the silver glow. Cornelius felt a twinge of unease when he realized how shaken his fellow SkyTalon looked. The feathers under Dustin's eyes were slightly more pale than the rest of his plumage, faint from the constant soaking of tears. His talons shook slightly, as if it was an effort just to stand. And his breathing came in shaky whispers.

Cornelius immediately felt a stab of guilt. *How did I not realize how broken he was?* he asked himself. *I could have helped him. I could have prevented this. Why didn't I do more?*

Cornelius, forcing down all of his fear, took a step closer to his friend. "I... I'm so sorry, Dustin," he told him. Cornelius wished that he could place a wing on his fellow SkyTalon's shoulder. But he couldn't bring himself to do it. The dark, blank look in Dustin's eyes scared him.

Cornelius drew in a deep breath. A thought had come to him. "It's because of your mother, isn't it?" he gently asked Dustin. "Is that why you hate the tribes so much?"

To his surprise, the smallest tear fell from Dustin's eyes. The blue jay said nothing, so Cornelius continued on.

"You want to destroy the Life Tree because she lost her life defending it," he murmured. "You blame the tree, and the tribes, for your pain. That's why you want to get back at them."

Cornelius felt his heart twist with pity. "Oh, Dustin," he whispered. "Please don't do this. This isn't you. You aren't a murderer. You're a SkyTalon, just like Shadow and I."

Dustin's eyes abruptly flashed with anger. "If you think I'm anything like you," he spat, "then I guess you don't know me very well at all!" His feathers began to flare. "I'm not just doing this to get back at

175

the tribes. There's more to it than that. I'm doing it to get revenge on Jarquanzila!"

Cornelius flinched, surprised. "What?" he breathed.

"Jarquanzila is *evil*, Cornelius," Dustin hissed. "Can't you see that he's just using all of us? He doesn't really care about the tribes... or any of us!" He began to slowly circle Cornelius. "You, of all birds should know that. It wasn't Donovan who cursed you to be a SkyTalon. It was Jarquanzila himself."

Cornelius instinctively extended his talons.

"And my mother didn't really die defending the Life Tree," Dustin growled. "She died defending Jarquanzila. Without that monster's magic slithering around inside of the tree, it's just a dead husk of rocks. Every bad thing that happens to the tribes is just a product of Jarquanzila's greed."

Dustin came to a halt in front of Cornelius. "And if Jarquanzila is so caring and perfect, why does he let innocent birds like me suffer?" he asked. "I was just a hatchling when Jarquanzila did nothing to help my mother. And I know for a *fact* that that creature can temporarily take form outside of the tree. Why wouldn't he fight to save her? Why wouldn't he even try lifting a talon to help her? Oh, but I know why. Because he's a fraud!" Dustin's feathers rose and fell with every sharp, furious breath he took. "And why wouldn't he try to stop my father from *forcing* me into becoming a Speaker?"

Dustin thrusted his beak forward. "Why would he ruin *your* life?" he demanded. "I know what I said earlier may have been cruel. But it's the truth. You don't belong here, Cornelius. The tribe's fight shouldn't have to be your fight." His eyes softened with regret. "You should be home, with your family and friends. Don't let Jarquanzila take you from that." Dustin dropped his gaze. "Don't die because Jarquanzila told you it was your destiny. Don't die because of me. Please."

Cornelius felt tears fall from his orange eyes. "You sound so much like Khan," he whispered, terrified.

Dustin nodded, something in his gaze brightening. "Yes, now you're beginning to understand!" he exclaimed. "Khan is a hero. He was the one who saved me in Jajarii!"

Dustin took a step closer. Cornelius immediately tensed up. He let out a warning cry, extending his talons. Cornelius was surprised by how scared he was around his own friend... if Dustin was even his friend to begin with.

"Jarquanzila had left me there to rot, Cornelius. He wasn't even going to try to save me," Dustin continued. "Khan was the one who helped me. Khan was the one who showed me how I could be free of my pain. It's because of him that I now have the power of shadows." Dustin let out a cold, joyless laugh. "It's ironic, isn't it. My power comes straight from Jajarii itself... from Jarquanzila. His own magic will be used, by me, to destroy him. What a perfect end to this story!"

Cornelius felt dread pour over him. "You don't have to do this," he pleaded. "Khan is just as manipulative as Jarquanzila. Whatever he told you... whatever he promised you... it's all lies. He isn't your real friend. Shadow and I are. We can really help you. We'll work this out, together."

Dustin let out a furious hiss. "And where were you when I needed you?" he snapped. "I tried to make you understand, when I had visited you in your dream all of those nights ago. And what did you do!? You rejected me!"

Dustin began to dangerously prowl closer. With every step he took, more and more shadows began to slide over Dustin's blue feathers.

"Khan actually took the time to listen to me! To understand me!" Dustin yelled. "He isn't the heartless monster you all accuse him of being. Sure, he's done terrible things before in the past. But what bird hasn't?" He shot a loathing look at Cornelius. "If I remember the stories correctly, didn't you and Shadow drop a whole *avalanche* on top of Aquila and those other ravens?"

Cornelius felt his heart shatter. "We couldn't save them..." he whimpered, the words catching in his throat.

Dustin's eyes widened.

"Oh really?" he pressed. "You tried to snap them out of their shock? You tried to do everything you could? I don't think so! You only worried about yourselves. And don't even try to deny it!"

Cornelius hung his head, feeling shame pulse through him. Guilt ravaged his heart. *Dustin's right,* he grimly told himself. *I know that I could have saved them. And yet I didn't.*

More and more shadows began to slide over Dustin's feathers, until he became completely covered by them. The once small blue jay now towered over Cornelius. He looked double the size of a no-feather in the city. Fear rushed through Cornelius' veins.

"This is your final chance," Dustin warned. "Join me now, or leave the tribes forever. Because if you don't, it'll be the *end* of you, along with everything, and everyone."

Cornelius felt his heart rapidly pound. This was his chance to save himself. This was his chance to go home. *But I'd rather die than be a coward,* he told himself. Slowly, Cornelius lifted his head, forcing himself to meet the Shadow Within's gaze. "Do your worst," he spat.

Dustin, without a moment's hesitation, extended his black talons. He lashed them forward, toward Cornelius. The small pigeon slammed his eyes shut. The world around Cornelius flashed white.

Cornelius gasped, opening his eyes. He found himself back in the Blue Jay Tribe, in the waking world. He was right where he had fallen asleep, on one of the many tree branches high above the forest floor. Panic gripped Cornelius, and he jumped to his talons.

"Dustin!" he screamed as loudly as he could. "Dustin is the Shadow Within! Dustin is–"

Cornelius' words were cut off as a heavy weight exploded into him. The breath was knocked out of his chest. Cornelius was sent spiralling off the branch. He was plummeting toward the ground!

With a ghastly screech, Dustin dove down to meet him, talons outstretched and rage burning in his eyes.

# CHAPTER 27

Branches whipped against Cornelius as he cannoned down to the ground. Hot pain seared through him. He was upside-down, his wings thrashing helplessly. Fear rushed through Cornelius. *I'm so high above the ground,* he realized, beginning to panic. *A fall from this height... No, I won't let that happen! I have to fight!*

Dustin exploded downward to Cornelius. In the waking world, he didn't have his coat of shadows. But he didn't need it. The Shadow Within would destroy Cornelius with his bare talons. Dustin extended his pointed claws, gaining a frightening burst of speed. Malice sparkled in his blue eyes.

Cornelius winced as Dustin slashed his talons through his side. Grey feathers were sent spiralling away in the rush of wind. Then, Dustin clamped his talons around the plumage on Cornelius' neck. He added a deadly amount of weight, causing Cornelius to plummet even faster than before.

"Stop it," Cornelius pleaded. He warily eyed the rising forest beneath them. "It isn't too late!"

A cold, joyless smirk appeared on Dustin's face. "Oh, how right you are, Cornelius," he chuckled. "This is only just the beginning!" Dustin, with one talon still fiercely gripping Cornelius' neck, reared up for another attack. Dustin lifted his other talon, each thorn-sharp claw dangerously extended.

Just before the Shadow Within could strike, Cornelius rolled in the air, causing himself to rapidly spin out of control. He felt dizzy as the sky quickly swapped places with the ground, over and over again. Dustin was dislodged immediately. He let out a shriek of defiance, then swiftly rushed over to continue the fight.

The two birds crashed to the ground in a whirl of gashing beaks and slashing talons. They were desperately trying to overthrow the other. Because if they didn't, they would hit the ground, and everything they worked so hard for would be over in an instant.

Cornelius, just barely avoiding Dustin's talons, shot a horrified glance at the ground below. The pigeon felt his heart beat out of his chest. They were only seconds away from crashing!

In that brief moment of distraction, Cornelius accidentally allowed himself to get caught up in Dustin's talons. The blue jay, with all of his strength, latched his claws around Cornelius' wings. Dustin wouldn't let himself get thrown off a second time!

Pain rushed through Cornelius' sensitive wings as Dustin cruelly dug into them.

"Goodbye, Cornelius," Dustin snarled. "I wish I could say that it didn't end with us being enemies. But you had your chance, and you tossed me aside, just like everyone always does." He jabbed his talons even deeper into Cornelius' wings. Anger and determination glowed in Dustin's eyes. "I'm going to do whatever it takes to avenge my mother. No bird is going to take that away from me! Not even you."

Cornelius felt regret rush through him. As he gazed up at his friend, he realized that he barely even recognized him anymore. Dustin looked so angry... so broken.

"I'm sorry," Cornelius choked out.

Dustin's eyes flashed with surprise.

"I'm so, so sorry," Cornelius continued. "You didn't deserve this. Any of this. I was a bad friend." His voice broke as he spoke. "You needed my help so much, and yet I didn't even once notice how much pain you were in. I should have been there for you, Dustin. It should never have come to this."

Dustin had to force back angry tears, refusing to let Cornelius see him cry.

"I won't make excuses for my mistakes," Cornelius told him. "Do what you want to me. I deserve it. But the tribes don't. No bird meant to cause you harm. No bird wanted you to suffer."

Dustin dropped his gaze, unable to look at him.

Cornelius gave the forest floor one last glance. It was just a few feather lengths away from him now. Wind screeched through Cornelius' ears and buffeted his feathers. But he barely even noticed it. All Cornelius felt was dread. *I failed Dustin, and the tribes,* he thought. *And now everyone will suffer.*

Cornelius closed his eyes, ready for the end.

Suddenly, he felt a weight crash into his side. Cornelius gasped as the breath was knocked out of his chest. He threw open his eyes and watched as he tumbled to the forest floor. Pain exploded through

Cornelius as he uncontrollably rolled. He finally came to a halt as he crashed into the trunk of a tree.

Cornelius watched dizzily as Dustin slammed into the ground a wing's length away from him. He couldn't believe it. *Dustin saved me,* Cornelius blearily realized. *He crashed into me so that I wouldn't hit the ground head-on. But what did it cost him?* Pain and fear surged through Cornelius as he gazed at the unmoving shape of Dustin.

Cornelius shakily rose to his talons. He swayed as he slowly limped forward, but continued on nonetheless. His vision blurred as he collapsed right in front of Dustin. Cornelius reached out a trembling, blood stained wing to prod his friend. "Please wake up," he murmured weakly. "You can't go. Not like this."

Dustin's eyes slowly opened.

Cornelius felt a rush of relief. "You saved me," he whispered, not having the strength to make his voice any louder. "Why?"

Before Dustin could answer, blue jays began to rush forward. They surrounded the two SkyTalons. Their shouts of concern rang in Cornelius' ears, and his vision began to fill with dancing, black stars. He managed to glimpse the blurry shape of Elizabeth, Dustin's aunt. She pushed through the crowd, closely followed by another Healer. Elizabeth, focused exclusively on Dustin, ordered the other Healer to go to Cornelius.

Cornelius felt his heart skip a beat as Elizabeth moved closer to Dustin. "Stop!" he screamed with all of the energy he had left. "Stay away from him! Dustin's the Shadow Within!"

Cries of terror exploded through the crowd. The tribe was plunged into chaos. Blue jays immediately began to flee, moving as far away from Dustin as they could. Elizabeth stood firm, although fear flashed in her eyes. She opened her beak to speak, but then quickly closed it as Atticus came to land beside her.

Dread was etched in the leader's gaze. "What is the meaning of this?" Atticus demanded, voice strained with worry. "What has happened?"

"Cornelius says that Dustin is the Shadow Within," Elizabeth told Atticus in disbelief. The Healer's attention then snapped to Dustin. "Please tell me this isn't true," she pleaded to her nephew. "Tell me that Cornelius is mistaken." When Dustin didn't answer, Elizabeth staggered a few paces backward, eyes growing wide.

Atticus froze. His feathers slowly began to spike out. "No," he whispered. Atticus suddenly looked sick as he dragged his gaze onto Dustin. "No, it can't be. I-I didn't want to believe it. I didn't want t-this to happen."

Dustin's eyes were blank and glazed, staring emptily ahead. Cornelius looked at him nervously. At first, he thought that Dustin had gone unconscious from the shock and pain of the fall. Then, the small blue jay slowly stirred.

Dustin's eyes travelled upward as he looked at the far side of the camp. Then, he let out a weak laugh. "Oh, but it's *because* of you that this happened," Dustin murmured to Atticus. "If you hadn't forced me into becoming a Speaker, I never would have met Khan. I never would have gotten the power I needed to destroy each and every one of you."

Cornelius followed Dustin's gaze, the ground swaying from underneath him. Then, he felt his blood run cold.

Past the chaos of the scrambling Blue Jay Tribe, hidden deep inside of the shadows of the forest beyond the camp, was an army of seagulls.

When Cornelius turned to look back at Dustin, a chilling smile had appeared on the blue jay's face. Cornelius felt a stab of fear when he noticed that Dustin's gaze was fixed directly on him. "I told you, Cornelius," he shakily said. "This is only just the beginning."

"Attack!" Jerimiah, the leader of the seagulls, screeched. The command sliced through the tribe like a talon. And for a brief second, the forest was plunged into silence.

In the blink of an eye, the camp became flooded by vicious, revenge-driven seagulls. Screams of fear exploded from the unprepared blue jays.

Darkness wrapped its chilling wings around Cornelius' eyes, and the world went black.

# CHAPTER 28

Cornelius gasped, drawing in a massive breath. With a jolt, he scrambled to his talons and looked around. Cornelius froze, startled. This wasn't the Blue Jay Tribe.

In front of him, darkness. Behind him, darkness. Everywhere he looked, there was nothing but an eerie veil of blackness. Cornelius shivered, shrinking inside of his feathers. He hated it. He hated having nothing but the company of emptiness. He hated feeling so alone.

Suddenly, a thought struck him. How could he have forgotten? *The tribe!* Cornelius remembered, panicked. *They're in danger. The seagulls and Dustin will destroy them!*

Cornelius quickly scanned the area, desperate to find some way out of this void. *What is this place? Jajarii? I can't be here!* Fear slithered through his feathers. *I have to go back to the tribe and save them!* Cornelius' heart began to race.

"Jarquanzila?" he called out. Was the spirit finally about to end his silence, and tell Cornelius how he could restore peace to the tribes? Cornelius stood in silence for a moment, waiting for an answer. But that answer never came.

Cornelius froze. Nervousness crawled beneath his plumage. Something felt different about Jajarii this time. *The air isn't freezing,* Cornelius realized. He hurriedly waved a wing in front of his face and let out a gasp. Cornelius could see it! *That's next to impossible to do inside of Jajarii,* he thought. Cornelius gulped, coming to the realization that he wasn't inside of Jarquanzila's abyss.

So then, where was he now?

Suddenly, the smallest glimmer of light appeared far in the distance. Cornelius almost missed it. He paused, watching it carefully. *If this place isn't connected to Jarquanzila, and if he isn't here, then who... or what... is that?* Cornelius wondered nervously. Were there more guardian spirits out there, other than Jarquanzila himself? Cornelius shivered, finding the thought oddly chilling.

Cornelius hesitated for a moment, looking at the twinkle of light in apprehension. Part of him was curious to discover what this strange spirit wanted. Another part of him wanted nothing to do with it. But Cornelius had no choice. His only hope of leaving this void was to talk with this spirit, and see what it wanted. Cornelius, forcing down his fear, unfolded his wings and began to fly toward the light.

As Cornelius flew closer, the larger and brighter the light became. It glowed in a strangely inviting and comforting way. Cornelius found it familiar, in a sense. There was just something about it that he recognized, although he had no idea what. He quickly shook the thought away. *Stop being silly, Cornelius,* he scorned himself. *You're just imagining things.*

The white light gently danced in the darkness, and softly twinkled in Cornelius' eyes. He stared at it, but no matter how hard Cornelius looked, he just couldn't make out any details of a bird-like spirit inside of the glow.

A shiver ran down Cornelius' spine, and he quickly pulled himself into a hover.

Despite how peaceful this spirit seemed, Cornelius just couldn't bring himself to trust it. Not until Cornelius knew that it was safe to do so. *I won't let myself trust anyone like I used to,* he told himself. Cornelius felt his heart twist with grief. *Not like I did with Dustin.*

Cornelius dove to the black ground below, landing as silently as he could. Then, he lingered just a few wing lengths away from the light. Cornelius shifted uneasily on his talons, worry worming beneath his plumage. *I don't think the spirit knows that I'm here,* Cornelius realized.

Frustration began to burn beneath his plumage. *I'm wasting time just standing here,* Cornelius thought. *Who knows what horrors are going on in the Blue Jay Tribe? I need to get this spirit's attention right away, so that I can leave this place.*

"Hello?" Cornelius whispered, the word dying off in his throat as he said it.

The spirit didn't react.

Cornelius, forcing himself to be brave, lifted his head and faced the light. "Hello?" he repeated, louder this time. "I'm here now, like I think you want me to be. Can we please talk?"

Suddenly, the light began to grow brighter, and brighter, and even brighter than before. In a matter of seconds, it began to fill up the entire space, leaving not even a single trace of darkness behind. Eyes burning, Cornelius tightly wrapped his wings around his face.

After a few seconds, Cornelius could sense the blinding light beginning to subside. He wavered for a moment, then gingerly folded his wings back. Cornelius opened his eyes. He immediately let out a startled gasp, disbelief pulsing through his veins. Cornelius took a step backward. *It's my flock's camp in the city,* he realized.

It was just how Cornelius remembered it to be. Cozy, yet cramped. Boring, yet interesting in just the right amount. Empty... wait. It was never empty. Where was everyone? Cornelius scanned the camp, starting to feel worried. Then, he felt his breath snag in his throat. Shock and terror surged through Cornelius, making him feel faint.

Where the pile of cardboard boxes should have been, now rested a pile of ash. The concrete around it was black, burnt, destroyed. Feathers were scattered all over the ground. Cornelius felt sick as he studied them more carefully. He recognized feathers that would have belonged to Jemma, Xavier, Corra, Adrea, Harrison, and many others. But there were a few dark brown feathers that belonged to a pigeon that Cornelius had never seen before.

Cornelius felt his head reel. Something very bad had happened here, and he could only dare to imagine what.

Instinctively, Cornelius extended his talons. *None of this can be real,* he thought. *It must be Dustin or Khan playing a trick on me. Dustin did something like this before. He could be doing it again now.*

Cornelius' heartbeat began to quicken. Deep down, he knew that what he was seeing now was the truth. Cornelius' home in the city had been destroyed. He was too horrified to cry. He was too stunned to look away. All Cornelius could do was stare.

*Click.*

The sound was so silent that Cornelius had almost missed it. He whirled around, talons extended and ready for the first sign of danger. Cornelius felt his heart skip a beat as he found himself gazing into the eyes of another pigeon. One that he recognized. One that was so much like him. One that he knew well... or thought that he had known well. Cornelius staggered slightly, the world swaying from under his talons. "No," he breathed, shocked.

Donovan smiled at him. "Hello, grandson."

Cornelius took a step backward, quivering. "You aren't real," he shakily said, more to himself than to the transparent shape of his grandfather. "This is just a dream. This is all just in my head."

Donovan's smile dropped ever so slightly. "I wish I could say that it was," he began. "But I am very much real. And so is all of this." He pointed to the scorched concrete wall.

Cornelius suddenly felt sick as a thought came to him. "You're the spirit... aren't you?" he choked out. Donovan hesitated before offering a small nod. Cornelius felt tears trickle from his eyes. "So that must mean that you..."

Donovan walked over to Cornelius and wrapped his wings around him. Cornelius buried his head deep inside of his grandfather's plumage, sob after sob gripping him. "I missed you so, so much, grandfather," Cornelius murmured. For just a moment, he managed to forget about Donovan's betrayal to the tribes, and to him.

But that moment didn't last long.

Cornelius broke away from his grandfather, looking at him bitterly. "You used me," he began. "And you betrayed Atticus and

Ellagard, your friends. How could you do that to them... to me? I trusted you with every feather I had on me. I thought we didn't keep secrets from each other."

Donovan looked grim. "Some secrets are better left buried, Cornelius," he replied. "The truth can be a deadly thing." Donovan reached out a wing to place on Cornelius' shoulder.

Cornelius recoiled, moving away from him. Donovan let out a sigh before continuing. "I wish I can be honest with you, and tell you the real story of what happened."

Cornelius felt a stab of annoyance. "Then do it," he insisted through a gritted beak. Anger suddenly bubbled in his chest. "Haven't you kept enough secrets from me? Why keep me in the dark, even now when you have nothing to lose?" Before Donovan could answer, Cornelius continued on. "If you ever cared about me, even for just a moment, then you'll just let me know what's going on!"

Donovan was silent for a very long moment. "I'm sorry," he said. "But I can't tell you the truth."

Cornelius felt his heart shatter.

"You may think that I'm cruel, and you have every right to think that," Donovan continued flatly. "But I can assure you, every terrible thing I've done is to save the tribes. Even by leaving them, I was helping them in ways that you will not understand."

Cornelius, forcing back angry tears, locked gazes with his grandfather. "So why are you here now?" he asked, keeping his voice as steady as he could. "If you don't care about me, why even waste time talking to me?"

For just a moment, sorrow flashed in Donovan's blue and green eyes. But that moment didn't last long, and he returned to his distant, cold self. "To deliver a warning," Donovan answered. He closed his eyes and drew in a deep breath. "Chaos will ravage through the tribes. We must rely on those who lie. Darkness is only just a disguise. Trust everyone, yet no one at all. Trust in yourself, or else all will fall."

Cornelius paused, confused. He opened his beak to question his grandfather, then let out a yelp of surprise. In the blink of an eye, Donovan vanished, leaving Cornelius all alone. Cornelius' ruined home began to darken away into nothingness. "Wait!" he cried. "Don't go yet! I still need answers!"

But it was no use. In a matter of seconds, Cornelius was plunged back into the waking, living world. He opened his eyes and found himself in the same spot where he had blacked out.

Dustin was nowhere to be seen.

The sky was as red as the blood scattered on the ground around Cornelius. Birds were viciously fighting all over the tribe. Feathers littered the camp—some from seagulls and others from blue jays. And in the distance, hanging above all of the fighting, was a full moon. Soon, it would be in the center of the sky, and Dustin would be at his full power.

A ghastly screech suddenly tore through the noise. Cornelius looked up, then felt his blood turn to ice. Jerimiah dove down to him with startling speed. Rage burned in his eyes. The seagull's talons were extended, ready to tear Cornelius to shreds.

# CHAPTER 29

Ellagard let out an annoyed hiss as she almost tripped into a puddle of mud. Muttering under her breath, she dislodged her talon from the surfaced, arch-like tree root. Dust and dirt clung onto Ellagard's feathers, making her plumage look more brown than blue. But despite her exhaustion, she kept on moving forward. Ellagard refused to let Zander down a second time!

The sun blazed high in the sky, making the jungle below feel stuffy and hot. *Before I left the tribe to start my journey to Misty Falls, the sun had only just started to rise,* Ellagard remembered. *Now, the sun will be setting shortly. Will I make it to rogue territory before nightfall?*

Ellagard paused to catch her breath. She suddenly felt a stab of regret. *Maybe I should have taken Reyna's advice and let her come along,* Ellagard thought, frowning. *It sure would be nice to have another peacock with me for support.* She sighed. *I was in such a hurry to rescue Zander that I didn't even stop for a moment to think. Have I gone crazy? I'm about to sneak into Misty Falls, the rogue's very base, all on my own. I'm kidding myself if I think that I'm going to make it out of there alive.*

Ellagard suddenly felt dizzy with worry. *Should I turn back now to get reinforcements, while I still have the chance?* she asked herself. *No. I'm not risking my Protector's lives for just one bird.* Ellagard dropped her gaze and looked at her talons. *But should I also be risking my life for just one bird?* Ellagard quickly shook the thought away, feeling disgusted with herself. *Of course I should. Zander is my friend. I owe it to him to try and save him, even if it means that I go down fighting.*

Determination flowing through her veins, Ellagard continued on. But every time she took a step, pain shot up her legs. Her mud-baked feathers felt as heavy as boulders as the sun scorched down onto her. Ellagard's breathing came in sharp gasps as she inhaled the hot, breezeless air. *Jarquanzila help me,* she thought weakly as a groan escaped her beak.

Ellagard suddenly stopped dead in her tracks. A prickle of unease crawled down her spine. Something was wrong.

For the first time, Ellagard noticed how silent the jungle was. Not even a cricket dared to chirp in the shaded undergrowth. There seemed to be no other creatures here, other than her. Ellagard scanned the trees for a monkey, looked up to the sky for the colourful wings of a butterfly. But, just as she expected, there were none to be seen.

Ellagard slowly extended her talons, fear beginning to rise in her chest. Part of her expected the rugged figure of Khan to come slinking out of the shadows at any moment. Another part of her expected a group of hungry ocelots to leap down from the trees and attack her.

Ellagard carefully scanned the jungle in front of her. It was free of any threats. Then, she looked behind her.

"Surprise!" a voice cheered.

Ellagard nearly jumped out of her plumage.

Reyna stood only a feather's length away from her, grinning. Playful mischief sparkled in her yellow eyes. "Hi, Ellagard!" Reyna exclaimed. Then, she caught sight of Ellagard's weary eyes and disarrayed feathers. "Yikes, what happened to you? Did you trip into some mud or something?"

Ellagard felt her feathers bristle with embarrassment. "Yes, but only once," she mumbled. *And it almost happened far too many times after,* Ellagard thought.

Reyna nearly fell over laughing.

Ellagard clenched her beak. "Why are you here, anyways?" she snapped. "I told you to stay and lead the tribe while I'm gone. Who's doing that now?"

Reyna rolled her eyes. "You worry too much," she teasingly commented. "Your brother, Cyprus, of course. I asked him if he would like to lead while I'm gone. He asked me where you were, and I said not to worry about it." Reyna winked at Ellagard. "I knew you wanted to keep this mission a secret. And a secret it is. Anyways, Cyprus eventually agreed. So now he's temporarily leading the camp. And now we're free to go and rescue Zander. Hooray!"

Ellagard couldn't believe her ears. "No, not 'hooray'!" she snapped. "You shouldn't have done that, Reyna. I told you to stay for a reason. If I got captured or worse, the tribe would have had you for leadership. But now with both of us gone..." Ellagard buried her head in her wings, groaning.

"Pfft, you're acting like we won't make it back to the tribe," Reyna said nonchalantly. "Everything's going to be fine. I thought this all through before I left. The plan will continue as normal. You'll sneak in and hopefully find Zander. Then, you'll escape and everything will be fine. Say it doesn't go according to plan, however. No worries. Because now I'll be there to step in and save your feathers if any rogue catches you." Reyna encouragingly nudged her.

Ellagard let out a defeated sigh. "I know it'll be no use to try and reason with you," she murmured, folding her wings back. "So if you really insist on coming," Ellagard smiled at Reyna, "then I'll be happy to have a friend by my side."

"Oh, stop it, you," Reyna joked. "Come on. We can be all sappy later. We have a tribemate to save!"


The sound of crashing water grew louder and louder with every step Reyna and Ellagard took. The noise echoed through the silent jungle and filled their ears. They were now on the outskirts of rogue territory.

Ellagard felt a twinge of unease. Her heartbeat began to quicken. Instinctively, she stopped walking. Reyna quickly copied. "What should we do now?" Ellagard whispered to her, even though they were still a safe distance away from Misty Falls and any rogues.

Reyna shrugged. "You're the tribe leader, not me," she whispered back. "This is your call. You're going to be the peacock sneaking into the rogue's base, not me."

Ellagard frowned, then looked away from Reyna. Through the jungle's thick foliage and many intertwining branches, Ellagard managed to catch a glimpse of the massive hill of Misty Falls. It loomed ominously in the distance.

Millions of thoughts began to swirl in Ellagard's head. What if Zander was being guarded? What if she got spotted before she could even reach him? What if he was in no state to flee Misty Falls with her? What if, what if, what if...?

Reyna, sensing Ellagard's distress, gently placed a wing on her shoulder. "Everything is going to be okay," she gently told her. "We've got this together." Reyna lifted her head. "What if we scout the territory first? If we can catch a glimpse of..."

Ellagard blinked, confused. With every word Reyna spoke, the quieter and quieter her voice became. Within seconds, the crashing of the waterfall and Reyna's words were snuffed out. Ellagard was left in complete silence.

"Ellagard?" a soft voice called out. It sounded strange, wispy, and dreamlike.

Ellagard felt her heart skip a beat as she realized that the voice belonged to Zander. "Yes, it's me," she quickly responded. "Don't worry, I'm here. I'm coming right away."

"Ellagard, you have to hurry," Zander urgently told her. "Time is running out. I don't know how much longer I can last. I'm on the very top of Misty Falls."

Ellagard froze. "Are there rogues close to you?" she asked. "Do you think that I can sneak up there unnoticed?"

"Yes, but only if you come right away," Zander pressed. "All of the rogues are gone for now. I don't know why, or where. Even Khan isn't here. But I know that they'll be back soon." He suddenly gasped, as if in pain. "Please, hurry!"

Without warning, the crash of the waterfall returned. The sudden noise sliced through Ellagard's ears like merciless talons, causing her to flinch.

Reyna was motionless, with concern brimming in her eyes as she gazed at Ellagard. "What just happened?" she asked. "Who were you talking to? Is everything alright?"

Ellagard took a step away from Reyna. "I'm sorry, but there isn't time to explain!" she told her. "Now is my only chance to rescue Zander. Stay here. I'll be back soon."

Without giving Reyna a chance to protest, Ellagard turned her back on her and began to ran. Ellagard didn't hesitate as she broke through the cover of the trees, and into the clearing beyond. Ellagard trusted Zander's judgement. If he said that there were no rogues to worry about, then Ellagard wouldn't waste time by being cautious. She refused to let Zander be trapped with those traitors for a second longer!

As Ellagard began to climb up the tall hill of Misty Falls, she felt a prickle of concern. *Zander didn't stretch the truth,* she realized. *There are no rogues anywhere. I wonder where they all went. Not to my tribe, that's for sure. Zander would have realized if they were planning another invasion, and told me about it.*

Excitement began to pulse through Ellagard's plumage as she ran. She was almost at the top of the hill! Despite her legs screaming in protest with every movement she made, Ellagard forced herself to climb even faster than before. *I'm coming, Zander!* she wordlessly told him.

She climbed higher and higher. Faster and faster!

Then, with a massive leap, Ellagard was at the very peak of Misty Falls. "Hello?" Ellagard called out between laboured breaths. "Zander? I'm here now."

"Oh, thank you, Ellagard," came Zander's voice.

Ellagard turned to her side, following the direction of his words, then let out a gasp of joy. Happiness surged through her when she caught sight of him.

Zander was perched on a small tree. His turquoise feathers were striking against the blood-red sunset sky behind him. His long tail feathers hung lazily beneath him, swaying slightly in the wind. And his green eyes were all on Ellagard.

Ellagard ran forward to greet him, feeling relief and joy wash over her. Then, she stopped dead in her tracks. Ellagard felt her heart skip a beat as another peacock stepped forward, sliding out from behind the tree. Ellagard's blood turned to ice as she caught sight of his countless scars. His dark plumage. His eerie, glowing amber eyes.

"Hello, sister," Khan said, a smile creeping over his beak. "I'm happy to see you again at last."

# CHAPTER 30

Cornelius let out a gasp as Jerimiah rushed toward him. With just a second to spare, Cornelius dodged to the side, just barely missing his webbed talons. Jerimiah was knocked off balance and slammed into the ground. But the seagull leader wasn't prepared to give up that easily. He quickly rose to his feet, then sprang at Cornelius.

Cornelius winced as he felt his grey feathers get torn out of his side. Jerimiah wasn't finished yet. He clamped his yellow beak around the plumage on Cornelius' neck, then roughly threw him to the ground. Pain surged through Cornelius.

"I'm sorry that it has to come to this, pigeon," Jerimiah rumbled as he walked over to the crumpled Cornelius. "But I know how important you are to the tribes. That friend of yours, Dustin, told me all about how you are a symbol of hope to them. By destroying you, I destroy their hope. And then they'll be that much easier to demolish."

"You don't have to do this," Cornelius gasped as Jerimiah began to sink his talons into his plumage. "I know that you want peace just as much as I do. But this isn't the way! Hurting birds isn't going to get you your home back."

Jerimiah rolled his eyes. "Trust me, if there was another way, don't you think we would have done it by now?" he spat. "I wish that my flock didn't have to sink as low as partnering with a traitorous, hot-headed blue jay to get what we want. But Dustin wants this tribe destroyed just as much as we do. And right now, there are no other options left."

Cornelius felt dizzy with pain as Jerimiah continued to dig his talons into him. "But this isn't right," Cornelius choked out. "I understand that your flock was wronged. And I understand that you must be in a lot of pain. But violence isn't going to solve anything."

Jerimiah loosened his grip ever so slightly.

"Dustin is manipulative and cunning," Cornelius continued. "I know that he promised to get you your home back. Don't believe him. By the time Dustin is finished getting his revenge on the tribe, he will have destroyed everything. The blue jays. The Life Tree. The forest. And most definitely the seagulls. All Dustin wants is revenge for the loss of his mother. And he blames *you*, and the rest of the seagulls, for his pain. Don't think for a moment that Dustin will spare your flock. The seagulls will be the first thing Dustin annihilates."

Cornelius paused for a moment to allow Jerimiah to take in his words. "Dustin doesn't care about anything other than vengeance," he pressed. "Can't you see that he's just using you to get what he wants?"

Jerimiah's feathers began to ruffle. "And how can I trust you?" he asked. "You side with the tribe, after all. How do I know that you aren't just trying to trick me?"

Cornelius steadily met Jerimiah's gaze. "You don't," he told him flatly. "You have no reason to trust me. But what I'm going to tell you now is the truth: if you and the other seagulls stop the battle, I will do everything in my power to help you get your home back. Without any more bloodshed. Without any more fighting. Without any more lies."

Jerimiah was silent for a long time. Deep down, he knew that what Cornelius was saying was the truth. Dustin *would* destroy every seagull in an instant, if he was allowed to rise to power.

Jerimiah then ran Cornelius' offer through his head, over and over again, considering all of the consequences that his decision might have for his flock. Jerimiah wanted this feud to end just as much as Cornelius did. And like Cornelius, he wanted to do it without another drop of blood being spilled, or another feather being pulled.

But what would it cost Jerimiah's flock if Cornelius was lying? What if Dustin really wasn't as vicious as Cornelius made him out to be? Was the risk worth their morals?

This could be the seagull's last chance to drive away the Blue Jay Tribe for good… to get their home back.

"Us seagulls aren't vicious," Jerimiah said at last. "But that Dustin has made us become birds that we aren't. Birds who are willing to hurt others just to get what we want. Birds who are prepared to drive away an entire tribe from their home."

Jerimiah let out a deep sigh. He stepped away from Cornelius, gently removing his talons.

"When you came to visit us all those countless days ago… your words touched me," the seagull murmured. "For the longest time, I was conflicted. Dustin offered us everything we wanted and more. But I knew, deep in my heart, that we would never be happy by destroying the Blue Jay Tribe. I didn't want to admit it to myself. I didn't want to know that all of these years of desire for revenge had been for nothing."

Jerimiah suddenly flinched as a loud shriek exploded above them. A seagull was sent crashing to the ground, after mercilessly being attacked by two blue jays. Cornelius and Jerimiah dodged to the side, just barely missing the plummeting seagull by a second. She collided to the ground with a sickening thud. The massive seagull then rose to her talons after a few seconds. She shot back into the air to continue the fight. All around Jerimiah and Cornelius were birds brutally fighting against one another. The forest was stained with blood, and feathers littered the ground. The camp was in ruins.

Jerimiah suddenly looked sick as he took in the battle. "What am I doing?" he whispered, aghast. "How could I have let this happen?" The seagull leader dragged his gaze down to his blood stained talons, his eyes growing as wide as the full moon in the distance. For a moment, all he could do was stare in a horrified silence. Then, Jerimiah slowly turned to look at Cornelius.

"I'm sorry," he choked out, distress oozing out of every word. "I'm so, so sorry."

Then, Jerimiah took in a deep breath to collect himself. He quickly became his calm, dignified self once more. "I'm sorry that you had to see the worst in us," Jerimiah continued. "My flock and I were just so angry. Just so bitter about the past. But I see now that we were only hurting *ourselves* by refusing to let go and move on."

Jerimiah drooped slightly. "The Blue Jay Tribe has been so loyal to protect the home that they've built for themselves," he murmured. "They never once tried to flee. Never once gave up. They truly care about this place... so who are we to take it all away from them?"

Cornelius shakily rose to his talons. "So what are you saying?" he whispered in disbelief.

Jerimiah steadily met Cornelius' gaze. "I'm saying that it's time to let go of the past, let go of our rage, and move on to something new. Something better," he replied. "The world is a huge place. There are more forests, more lakes, and more places to call our home out there. We don't have to stay tethered to this forest like we have for countless moons. By doing that, we keep on reminding ourselves of what we don't have, instead of what good things still lie ahead."

Cornelius felt his heart begin to pound. "But this was your home," he protested. "What happened to the seagulls was cruel. You shouldn't have to leave the forest."

Jerimiah shook his head. "I'm not having to, I'm choosing to," he explained. "The rest of my flock will be angry. Most of them will not understand. And it will take time to heal. But I know that in the end, letting go of our grudges will make us happier."

Jerimiah placed a wing on Cornelius' shoulder. "Thank you for helping me realize the truth," he said. "Now, go save the Blue Jay Tribe. Go make things right."

Jerimiah took a step back. Then, he let out an ear-splitting screech. "Seagulls!" he commanded, launching into the chilly air. "Retreat! This battle is over!"

Jerimiah's words were met by cries of confusion and disbelief. Some were from the seagulls, and others from the blue jays. Then, after a few seconds, the seagulls began to break away from the battle. They joined their leader in the air. Once every seagull had reunited, Jerimiah turned his attention onto Cornelius. He offered him a small nod.

Then, Jerimiah turned and flew out of the camp. The rest of the seagulls quickly copied. Cornelius watched, feeling strangely empty, as the last seagull vanished into the night.

The tribe was deathly silent for a long, long moment. Then, cries of victory exploded from the blue jays.

"We won!"

"The battle is over!"

"Cowards! Cowards!"

Cornelius felt a flash of alarm. *No, they got it all wrong,* he thought. *The seagulls aren't cowards! Doesn't the tribe see that the seagulls are being strong by letting go of their anger?*

Without warning, a slow, wicked laugh slithered through the ears of every bird. The hate rooted deep inside of the noise was enough to silence even the loudest of cheers. "Go ahead," a venomous voice called after the seagulls. "Try and flee, while you still can."

All heads turned to the direction of the voice. Then, blue jays began to flee. Screams of horror spilled into the night.

Dustin stood on a branch of the Life Tree. His wings were outstretched as he basked in the tribe's panic.

Atticus, Shadow and Elizabeth were crumpled on the ground. They looked up at Dustin in terror.

Inky, blobby shadows began to ooze out of the many small cracks in the Life Tree. They slithered up the stone-like tree, then creeped up

Dustin's feathers. It looked as though the darkness of Jajarii itself was taking form, and wrapping around the small blue jay.

Dustin soon became covered with shadows. Not even a single one of his dark blue feathers could be seen.

Dustin began to grow taller, and taller, and even taller than before. The branch that Dustin was perched on let out an awful groan, then snapped under the Shadow Within's weight. Dustin eerily glided up to the topmost branch of the Life Tree.

"You all took *everything* from me!" Dustin shouted to the fleeing tribe. His voice was loud enough to match the booming of thunder. "And now I will take away everything from *you!*" The Shadow Within tossed back his head and let out a series of terrible, twisted cackles.

Cornelius covered his ears with his wings, crumpling to the ground. Horror, panic, and fear seized him.

Dustin had won.

Cornelius had failed.

And now all of the tribes were doomed.

# CHAPTER 31

Another awful laugh slid out of Dustin's beak as the full moon shone behind him. Dustin's massive shadow loomed over the tribe, casting them into darkness. His blobby, black beak was twisted into a terrible, sickening grin. Dustin had everything that he always dreamed of. The world rested in his talons now. No bird stood in his way. No bird could stop him!

Shrill screams of panic were thrown into the night as the tribe continued to flee. Everywhere Cornelius looked was chaotic. Blue jays were flying, running, scrambling, doing everything they possibly could to escape the camp. Cornelius just barely missed colliding with a terrified, round-eyed Nathanial as he bolted past. The blue jay's wings desperately flapped as he flew. "Save us!" Nathanial begged, calling over his shoulder. "Please!"

Dustin watched the chaos enfold for a few moments longer. Then, he lifted up a shadow-masked talon into the air. His hollow, sunken black eyes narrowed as he glared at the Life Tree. "I hope you're seeing this, Jarquanzila!" Dustin spat. "And I hope you feel the same pain that you caused me!"

Then, he mercilessly slashed his talons into the Life Tree. With a sickening *crack*, a dozen or so branches were demolished. They snapped off the tree effortlessly when Dustin struck them, as if they were made from fragile icicles. A cloud of ancient dust was sent billowing into the bone-chilling breeze.

Cornelius felt his heartbeat quicken. But despite his terror, he unfolded his wings and flew over to the Life Tree island. *It's my duty to protect the tribes,* he thought, landing behind the looming shape of Dustin. *I'll do whatever it takes to save them. No matter what the risk is for me.*

Cornelius studied the scene carefully. Should he attack Dustin now? *No,* he decided. *It's too risky. I'll lose an advantage if I let him know that I'm here.* Cornelius ducked his head and then carefully hid behind a large, destroyed branch of the Life Tree.

Dustin laughed. "Oh my, this is much more fun than I thought it was going to be," he commented. Then, he slowly turned to fix his piercing gaze on Atticus. "And I owe it all to you, father! Because of your cruelty, I became strong. I became powerful. And it's all thanks to you that I can now destroy this pathetic, *disgusting* excuse of a tribe."

An empty, joyless smile appeared on the Shadow Within's face. "Allow me to show my gratitude." As fast as a snake, Dustin launched a talon forward. He snagged it around Atticus, then lifted him high into the night sky.

Cornelius froze, terrified.

"Dustin, stop!" Shadow pleaded.

But Dustin couldn't care enough to listen. Rage burned in his shadowy eyes. Dustin lifted Atticus higher and higher. He only stopped once father and son were face-to-face.

A long, silent moment passed. Dustin gritted his beak. "Have you nothing to say?" he snarled, his voice dangerously low. "You ruined my life. You turned me into the monster I am." Dustin's black feathers began to bristle. "Please, entertain me with whatever dumb excuse you have. Tell me why you were such a terrible father!"

Atticus met his son's gaze unflinchingly. "Because I only wanted to shield you from the truth," he replied.

Dustin let out a snort of amusement. "I haven't heard this one before," he mocked. "Please, continue."

Atticus released a deep sigh. "I never wanted to hurt you. I never wanted to make you upset," he told him. "But lying to you all these years seemed like the only way to protect you. I knew for a while that you were the Shadow Within. But I didn't think that you were as angry as you are, Dustin. Not enough to do all of *this*." Atticus grimly gestured to the destruction around him. "I wish that you never had to learn the truth. Not like this. But I just couldn't bring myself to tell you. Not after your mother and I made that promise."

Dustin froze. "What promise?" he demanded.

Atticus drooped like a withering plant. Sorrow filled his eyes. Then, lifting his head high and meeting his son's gaze, Atticus spoke. "I never wanted you to become a Speaker, Dustin," he stated. "It was never my choice. I *had* to make you do it." The tribe leader suddenly looked pained, as if a memory was hurting him.

"On the night when we... lost your mother, I found her in her final moments, on this very island," Atticus gently murmured, knowing how much this would hurt his son. "She was terrified of who would take her place as Speaker, once she was gone. I didn't know how I could have reassured her. There were no birds, young or old, who had what it took to become one. Every blue jay lacked the talent and commitment that every Speaker needs."

Atticus sighed. "She knew this as well as I did. And time was quickly running out. Your mother just couldn't bear to leave us, without knowing that the tribe would be in good talons," he explained sadly. "So, in a final act of desperation, your mother told me that you were the only bird that she could trust to take on the position. She had seen something in you the moment you had hatched. Dustin, she wanted *you* to become the next Speaker after her."

Atticus had to force back tears as he continued. "Your mother made me *promise* that I would never tell you the truth, Dustin," he whimpered. "She knew how much you admired her. And she also knew how much you wanted to become a Healer one day, like her sister Elizabeth." Atticus hung his head. "Your mother knew that you would be crushed if you ever found out the truth. So that's why I lied to you. That's why I was never there for you. Because I knew that if I wasn't cold and distant, I would tell you everything."

Atticus couldn't hold back his tears any longer. They streaked down his face as he spoke. "I wasn't there when you flew for the first time," the leader whispered, more to himself then to Dustin. "I ignored you when you were scared during thunderstorms, or needed some bird to talk to. I kept you from becoming a Healer, the thing you dreamed about since you hatched out of your egg. I never even told you how much I loved you." Atticus shook with emotion. "I... I was terrible to you, Dustin. And I'll never forgive myself for it."

Atticus quickly pushed his emotions back down. "I understand why you're angry with me," he told him. "So do what you want to me. I deserve it. But the tribe doesn't. I'm begging you, Dustin. Please, leave them in peace."

Atticus then paused for a long moment. He slowly lifted his head, then stared the Shadow Within straight in the eyes. "Your mother wouldn't want this," the blue jay leader told Dustin. "What would she think if she saw you now?"

Dustin froze, suddenly mortified. The terror on his face was horrific, and the fear in his black eyes made Cornelius feel sick. Dustin immediately released his grip on Atticus, half-aware of what he was doing, then stumbled a pace backward. "But... but I was doing this all for her!" Dustin stammered. "I was getting revenge for *her*!"

Shadow lifted her head. "No, Dustin," she called up to him. "You were getting revenge for yourself."

Dustin cringed. "But this is what I have to do," he choked out. "I'm putting things right. I'm making things better."

Sorrow filled Atticus' eyes. "Does this look better to you?" he asked his son remorsefully.

Dustin's eyes widened, and silence gripped the deserted forest. He stared at Shadow, Elizabeth, and Atticus, who were huddled together fearfully. They were battered, in pain from the wounds that Dustin had inflicted upon them earlier. Elizabeth was especially shaken. She trembled in fear, tears sparkling in her eyes as she gazed up at her nephew. Dustin saw this, and instinctively reached out a talon to comfort her.

Cornelius stiffened. Should he expose himself now, and defend the others? But there was nothing violent in Dustin's movement. Cornelius then quickly remembered how Elizabeth was like a mother to Dustin. And despite every terrible thing that had happened, the Shadow Within's love for his aunt had remained.

Elizabeth tensed up as Dustin approached, then shrunk back in her feathers. "Stay away from us!" she screamed, horrified. "Don't come any closer."

Dustin froze, then put his talon back down. He looked past the still lake, and into the camp beyond. The tribe was in ruins. The place where he had called *home* for his entire life, was in ruins.

Dustin glanced down at his shadow-masked feathers, then suddenly looked sick. "Wh-what am I doing?" he whispered, terror laced in every word. "How could I have let this happen?"

Dustin's breathing began to come in sharp gasps. "No," he whispered. "No, no, no!" He let out an anguished wail, the weight of his decisions finally crashing down onto him.

Mortified, Dustin extended his wings. The blobby shadows that covered him immediately began to melt away, like mud in the rain. After they slid off of Dustin's plumage, they slithered back into the many cracks of the Life Tree. And, as quickly as they had emerged, they were gone. Dustin was now an ordinary, small blue jay.

A tense moment dragged by.

Dustin suddenly buried his head in his wings, tears dripping from his eyes. His soft sobs filled the silent night.

Cornelius couldn't believe how pitiful and helpless the once powerful Shadow Within now looked.

Atticus, without hesitation, landed beside his son. Then, he gently placed a wing on Dustin's shoulder. Dustin's head shot up, and he looked at Atticus in surprise. "It's okay," Atticus comforted. "Everything is going to be okay."

Shadow, Elizabeth, and Cornelius watched wordlessly from a safe distance, each unsure of what to do next.

Without warning, Shadow's head jerked up. Her eyes grew wide. "Watch out!" she screamed.

It all happened so fast. In a flash, a blur of blue exploded by. Dustin and Atticus were knocked apart. An agonized cry tore through the still night.

Cornelius felt a stab of fear.

Dustin swayed on his talons. He gripped his throat with his wing. His breathing came in sharp, rattling gasps. Then, with a sickening thump, Dustin collapsed to the ground. Scarlet blood pooled around him, fleeing from the gash in the SkyTalon's throat. It sparkled eerily in the white moonlight.

Commander Myra stood over Dustin, her eyes glowing victoriously as she watched him take his final breaths.

# CHAPTER 32

"No!" Cornelius screamed, the word twisted with dread. Horror began to press around his feathers, making him feel numb. The forest began to grow dim, and soon the only sound that he could hear was the ringing of his own ears. The world swayed from under Cornelius' talons.

For a moment, all he could do was stare.

All he could do was stand there, petrified.

All he could do was watch his friend die.

Atticus' eyes were round with shock as they darted from Dustin to Myra. Then, they blazed with a terrible rage. The tribe leader leapt at Myra, driving her away from the limp shape of Dustin.

Cornelius quickly shook his head, forcing down his fear. There had to be something he could do to help Dustin. This couldn't be the end! Cornelius quickly unfolded his wings, then rushed over.

Cornelius landed beside Elizabeth and Shadow, who were huddled beside Dustin. Elizabeth looked at the wound on Dustin's throat in sheer terror. "You're a Healer," Shadow snapped at her. "If anyone can save him, it's you. Tell us what we can do! Please!"

Elizabeth looked mortified. Her talons began to tremble. "Nothing," she whispered in a small voice. "W-we can't save him. The wound is too d-deep."

Cornelius felt his feathers flare. "No!" he shouted. "We have to try. There has to be a way. Please... please..." Dread and desperation washed over Cornelius, causing him to stagger.

Dustin coughed, a small and weak shudder rippling over his plumage. His once blue feathers were stained in red, and his eyes were glazed. But they looked up at Shadow, Cornelius, and Elizabeth lovingly.

"I'm sorry," Dustin choked out. Tears slowly began to slide down his beak, landing on the ground with a soft *plop*. "I was wrong to do what I did... thought that I would make things better... you all didn't deserve it." Another cough seized Dustin. Then, he weakly smiled at them. "But I'm happy now," he murmured. "As happy as I've been in a long time."

Shadow's own tears began to flow.

"Stop it," she told Dustin. "You're acting like this is the end. But you can't leave us. We have to go and restore peace to the Peacock Tribe. We have so many more adventures to live. We..." She trailed off when Dustin took her wings in his.

"Thank you for always being so kind to me, Shadow," Dustin shakily said. "You were a good friend."

Then, Dustin turned to his aunt, Elizabeth. Before he could say anything, Elizabeth opened her beak and spoke. "I'm sorry that you went through all of this pain alone, Dustin," she said in between sobs. "I was always close to you, and yet I never even once realized how much you needed me. I should have been a better aunt. And I should have been a better sister to your mother. I failed her. Just like I failed you. I'm so, so sorry."

Dustin shook his head. "Please don't blame yourself," he whispered to Elizabeth. "This is no bird's fault other than my own. I'm the one who's sorry."

Then, Dustin turned his attention onto Cornelius, unsure of what to say. But the look in his eyes was enough to match that of a million words. "Thank you," Dustin eventually gasped out. "And I'm sorry. I'm so, so sorry."

There was a loud crash from behind them. Myra was thrown to the ground, landing with a sickening thud that echoed through the night. Atticus viciously pinned her down, digging his talons deep into her plumage. Rage and dread glowed in his eyes. "How could you!?" Atticus snarled. "I trusted you to be the Commander of the Protectors, and my deputy. You had everything that most birds wouldn't even be ambitious enough to dream about!"

Myra scoffed. "Not everything, Atticus," she spat back. "Use your head. What am I missing out of those titles? Oh, that's right. Being leader, obviously." Myra's eyes glowed malevolently. "I was happy enough for a while when you chose me as your deputy. But then I began to realize that I could do so much better than you as leader. You've always called me ambitious. You always encouraged me to do great things. So that's why I figured that, by becoming leader, I could turn the Blue Jay Tribe into the most feared tribe of them all."

Myra's gaze flickered to Shadow, and then her eyes narrowed into two cold slits. "You know; it was your own brother who was actually my inspiration for all of this," she told her.

Shadow froze, each of her feathers ruffling. Something in her eyes snapped.

"Malik may be as crazy as a hive of buzzing bees," Myra continued, "but not all of his ideas are bad. I liked where he was going with his plan to conquer the Barn Owl Tribe. So that got me thinking. What if I became leader, and made our tribe the most fearsome of all?"

Myra laughed. The cold sound slithered through Cornelius' ears. "For so long, the Blue Jay Tribe has been the 'peaceful' one," she spat, suddenly angry. "I'm sick of every other tribe always expecting us to help out with their issues. I'm sick of seeing my tribemates being taken advantage of." She turned her glare onto Atticus. "And I'm sick of *you* constantly being such a push-over! Always jumping to please the other tribes. So that's why I wanted to take matters into my own talons."

Myra looked at Dustin without a trace of guilt. "He's not the only one I had to take down in my mission to leadership," she boasted, prideful even while being pinned to the ground.

Atticus froze. Dustin, with the last of his strength, turned to look at her in disbelief.

"I thought that by destroying your mate, Atticus, you would snap and give up your leadership. But you already know how that went," Myra softly hissed. Her gaze slithered back onto Dustin. "I was always planning to take care of you next," she snarled at the dying blue jay, "but I could never find a good time to do it. I had to be careful. If I was too bold, I would be caught. And I just couldn't afford that. My leadership was too important."

Myra looked at Cornelius and Shadow. "And then you two showed up. I was terrified at first. I thought for sure the *legendary* and *almighty* SkyTalons would uncover what I did," she said mockingly. "So that's why I set you up with that patrol of weaklings. I was hoping the seagulls would do all of the work for me. But, of course, you three just *had* to survive."

Myra let out a soft growl of frustration. "But I wasn't prepared to give up on my tribe so easily," she continued. "I saw an opportunity with all of the chaos that this dumb 'Shadow Within' thing was causing. While everyone was busy scrambling to discover who the traitor was, I was busy making plans." She glared at Dustin. "I was waiting for the right moment to destroy you. So I kept my eye on you. And then, one fateful night, I saw you fly over to the Life Tree island. I wondered, why would he be going there when it isn't even time for a Speaker meeting? And then I watched as you destroyed a couple of branches on the Life Tree. It was clear that you were the Shadow Within."

Myra smirked. "I had gotten the most perfect plan," she said. "If I was the one who saved the tribe from the evil, vile Shadow Within, well, I'd be made leader for sure! I couldn't just let the tribe discover that Dustin was the traitor, however. Because he would've been exiled, and there would have been no glory in it for me." She rolled her eyes. "If I was going to get rid of Dustin, it needed to be when all hope was lost. When the tribe was on the brink of destruction. When I would be remembered as a hero for centuries! So I framed that wimp Alessandra for the act. She was getting on my nerves for a while. And I figured that there was no better way to shake her off my plumage."

Myra chuckled. "And now I'm about to complete my plan, after all this time!" she announced. "I have to thank you, Dustin, for doing most of the work for me. By wounding your companions so badly, you have made them that much easier to destroy. And soon, Shadow Within, you will be gone, alongside the others."

Dustin's eyes filled with dread. Myra couldn't help but laugh. "Oh, don't look so distressed," she teased him. "This is what you wanted, after all. Everyone destroyed, and your legacy being how you ruined everything. Sooner or later, my tribemates will return, and they'll see *me*, their hero, who saved them all from the monstrous Shadow Within. And as for the loss of the others... well... they'll just blame you for it, Dustin." Myra's eyes sparkled greedily. "And then I'll finally be leader. I'll finally have everything I've ever wanted."

Atticus shook with anger. "You're a monster, Myra," he spat. "I can't believe that after everything I've done to help you grow, you still weren't content." Atticus clenched his beak. Then, to Cornelius' shock, he released his grip on her and let her stand. "Get out," Atticus darkly said. "And never return."

Myra threw Atticus a mocking look. "Once a pathetic peacemaker, always a pathetic peacemaker," she spat. "I would expect nothing less from you, Atticus. In fact, I was counting on this." She immediately leapt at him with her talons mercilessly extended.

Shadow instantly rushed forward. She drove Myra away from Atticus with swipe after swipe from her talons. Then, with a final powerful blow, she sent Myra reeling to the edge of the island. "You're outnumbered, and overpowered," Shadow snarled. "If you're as smart as you think you are, then you'll leave. Your plan isn't going to work."

Myra glared at Shadow, hate glowing in her eyes.

"You must think that you're so noble," Myra mocked. "But deep down you'll always know how tainted your blood is. Any bird who is related to Malik is more of a monster than I am. If you think that you'll ever be free of him, then think again. Malik, and the mistakes that you've made, will haunt you forever."

Shadow stiffened, fear flashing in her eyes. Then, she pushed her emotions down and returned to her distant self. "Leave now, while I still allow it," she growled.

Myra hesitated for a moment. Her gaze darted to Atticus, Shadow, Cornelius, Elizabeth, and then Dustin. The realization that she wouldn't be able to win this battle hit her. She had underestimated them. Myra gritted her beak. "Don't think for a second that this is over," she muttered. "Keep your eyes open. Watch your backs. Because one day I'll return, and you will pay for keeping me from what I want."

Then, Myra leapt from the edge of the island and glided away into the inky night sky. Within moments, she was gone.

Dustin suddenly let out a whimper of pain, trembling. Atticus immediately rushed over to his son. The leader gasped, horrified.

When Dustin saw his father, happiness glowed in his eyes like an ember. "Goodbye," Dustin whispered. Then, the ember in his eyes died out. The small blue jay went limp.

Dustin, the third SkyTalon, was gone.

# CHAPTER 33

The morning was peaceful, and the sky above was a soft blend of yellow and blue. A gentle breeze ran through Cornelius', Shadow's, Atticus' and Elizabeth's feathers. The four birds hadn't dared to move from Dustin's side all night, still lost in their grief and regret.

Cornelius looked down at his friend and felt his heart twist. Dustin looked peaceful, as if he were only just sleeping. *How could I have let this happen?* Cornelius asked himself, feeling a pang of sadness. *I should have done more. I should have been a better friend. I should have prevented this.*

Cornelius couldn't bring himself to cry anymore. His eyes were dry, burning from the constant tears that had flown out of them all night. Cornelius suddenly remembered how his grandfather, Donovan, had visited him only a few nights before. *Grandfather may not still be in this world anymore,* Cornelius thought. *But he still lives on, in another way. Perhaps Dustin is experiencing the same thing. So wherever he is... I hope he's happy now. Maybe he's even reunited with his mother.* The thought made Cornelius smile, but only for a second.

Cornelius couldn't help but think about Donovan again. He had only visited Cornelius to deliver a warning. At first, Cornelius had thought that his message would have helped him to restore peace to the Blue Jay Tribe. But, looking back on Donovan's warning now, he realized that all of the conflicts within the Blue Jay Tribe had been resolved... even if they weren't done so with a happy ending.

So if that was the case... what was Donovan warning him about? Cornelius gulped, feeling a tremor of fear. His gaze instinctively travelled to the Life Tree. *The Peacock Tribe...* Cornelius realized nervously. Donovan's words echoed through his head: *"Chaos will ravage through the tribes. We must rely on those who lie. Darkness is only just a disguise. Trust everyone, yet no one at all. Trust in yourself, or else all will fall."*

Cornelius shook his head, as if doing so would clear his troubling thoughts. *Jarquanzila help us,* he thought. Then, Cornelius felt a stab of bitterness. *What am I even saying? Jarquanzila doesn't even seem to care. What if Dustin... and Khan... are right? What if Jarquanzila really is just a monster?*

Cornelius felt unease worm beneath his grey plumage. *Stop it, Cornelius,* he scolded himself. *You're thinking like Khan. Like a villain.* Cornelius' feathers began to ruffle. But it wasn't because of his concern with himself. Cornelius felt a pair of eyes burn into his plumage.

*Click.*

The sound was so silent that Cornelius had almost missed it. He instinctively jumped to his talons and whirled around. Fear pulsed through his veins. Was Myra back so soon, like she promised she would be? But when Cornelius turned around, he wasn't looking into the murderous eyes of Myra.

These eyes were green. Gentle. Slightly cautious.

And his feathers weren't blue. They were striking, pure white. Just like the colour of freshly fallen snow. He had a yellow beak that was gritted slightly, as if he were embarrassed. And his scaly yellow talon tapped nervously against the rocky ground of the island. The bright red comb above his beak rested on the top of his head, like a crown.

Cornelius took a step backward, shocked. Could it be? No. It was impossible. But what was in front of him was clear. Cornelius was looking at the true form of Jarquanzila himself. Not just a voice. Not just a flicker of light. But him.

Jarquanzila was a rooster.

Cornelius moved closer to Shadow, as he always did when he felt uneasy. *I can't believe it,* he thought, bewildered. *Jarquanzila is a rooster? I was expecting him to be some sort of legendary eagle or something. How... strange.*

Jarquanzila flinched slightly. Cornelius remembered with a jolt that Jarquanzila had the ability to hear other's thoughts. Cornelius quickly forced his mind to be as silent as possible, embarrassed.

Jarquanzila shook his head. "Stop it," he told them. "Don't try and spare my feelings. I already know how you all think about me. I was listening to your thoughts all night." The rooster released a heavy sigh. "And what you think about me is right. I am terrible. And I have been acting like a monster."

Jarquanzila looked at Cornelius and Shadow. "I am sorry for abandoning you when you needed me the most," he murmured. "I won't try to defend myself. For so long, I've only been thinking about what is best for me. But I realize now that there is so much more to the tribes then just my own gain. And it was Dustin who showed me that."

Jarquanzila dug his talons in and out of the pebbly shore underfoot. "But I'm done being selfish," he announced. "And I'm done hiding behind a void of darkness. It's time that I step up, and fight as hard as the tribes do for peace." Jarquanzila suddenly looked grim. "I know that what I've done in the past was horrible. But what I'm about to say now is the truth: I am sorry. And I am prepared to do *whatever* it takes to do what's right from now on. Nothing will stop me from that."

Jarquanzila's gaze travelled to Dustin. The spirit suddenly looked emotionless for a few seconds. Then, Jarquanzila began to walk over to Dustin. Atticus stiffened, extending his talons slightly. But he stopped and took a step back after Elizabeth shook her head at him.

"I'm ready to start making up for my mistakes," Jarquanzila told them. "Starting with Dustin. His time wasn't supposed to come yet. I see a dark future without him. My plan needs him to be here."

Jarquanzila paused for a moment, his eyes blank. Then, he lowered his head and touched the tip of his beak to Dustin's. Jarquanzila closed his brilliant green eyes.

Without warning, the undamaged branches of the Life Tree began to emit a soft, blue glow. Time appeared to reverse. The gash on Dustin's neck slowly started to seal itself. Then, as quickly as Myra had inflicted it, the wound was gone. Cornelius gasped, feeling surprise spark through him. Jarquanzila had healed Dustin!

But, did it work...? Jarquanzila took a few steps backward until he stood behind the others.

The world grew silent, as if it was holding its breath. Not even a breeze dared to dance by. All eyes were on Dustin.

Then, the small SkyTalon stirred. Dustin's eyes slowly fluttered open. They brightened when he saw his family, and immediately filled with tears of joy. Atticus and Elizabeth quickly wrapped their wings around Dustin, with Shadow and Cornelius quickly doing the same. Each bird happily laughed, at a loss for words. *Things worked out after all,* Cornelius thought, feeling a huge smile grow on his face.

Cornelius lifted his head, ready to thank Jarquanzila. But the mysterious spirit was nowhere to be seen. Cornelius blinked, then smiled, returning his attention to his friends. Dustin was back, and that was all that mattered to Cornelius right now.

*Thank you, Jarquanzila,* Cornelius thought, sure that the spirit was somewhere out there listening.

# CHAPTER 34

Ellagard stood rooted to the spot, feeling terror surge through her veins. Khan, her brother and greatest enemy, stood only a wing's length away from her. And in that moment, she realized with a stab of fear that Reyna wouldn't be coming to rescue her. *I told Reyna not to follow me,* Ellagard remembered, starting to feel sick. *So now I'm all alone.*

Ellagard dragged her gaze away from Khan, then turned it onto Zander. The turquoise peacock looked bored as his gaze flickered from Khan to Ellagard. "Zander," she began, "what is the meaning of this? You told me that Khan was away."

Zander rolled his eyes, his long, hanging tail feathers bristling slightly. "After all this time, you still scold me like I'm your naïve trainee," he hissed. "But in the end, I was the one who fooled *you.*" Zander leapt from his tree branch, then landed beside Khan. The young peacock smirked.

"That was a pretty convincing act we put on for you, wasn't it, Ellagard?" Zander taunted. "I knew how much my 'death' would break you. So that's why Khan and I decided to stage it that night." Zander laughed. "I can't take all the credit, however. Khan was the one who came up with the plan. All I had to do was, with his help, slip into your dreams and manipulate you into coming here."

For just the briefest of moments, Khan cringed, dropping his gaze. But the scarred peacock quickly hid away his emotions, and became cold and distant once more.

Ellagard took a step backward, feeling her heart fiercely pound against her ribs. "*Manipulate* me?" she echoed in disbelief. The world violently swayed from under her talons. "This was all just a lie? A trick?" Rage suddenly surged through her. "Zander, how could you?" Ellagard screamed, feeling the sting of betrayal. "I... I trusted you!"

Zander's gaze darkened. "And I trusted *you*, Ellagard," he retorted. "And what did you do? Abandon me. Leave me here alone, not even once thinking that I might have still been alive!" Zander, furious, slashed his talons through the dirt. "I didn't only fake my death to help Khan with his plans," he continued. "I did it to see what you would do. See if you truly did care about me. But, obviously, you don't. And maybe you never even did."

Ellagard couldn't believe her ears. "I thought that I watched you die," she protested, plumage bristling. "And I mourned for you. I cried for you. But, looking at the lying monster you turned out to be, I can't help but find myself regretting giving you the time of day!"

Zander let out an angry hiss. He threateningly extended his long tail feathers. Ellagard readied herself for battle.

Khan's eyes flashed with concern for a moment. "I told you that we didn't bring her here for a fight," he told Zander. "I think that it's time you go."

Zander was silent for a long, long moment. "Fine," he eventually said, folding his tail feathers back and smoothing his plumage. Zander shot Ellagard a malevolent glare. "Don't think that this is over," he spat. "Because one day, we'll meet again. And when we do, you'll be finished."

Zander's eyes hardened, as if a dark thought had come to him. Then, he turned his back on Khan and Ellagard, prowling down the hill of Misty Falls.

Khan watched him go, then turned his gaze onto Ellagard. Before he had a chance to speak, Ellagard leapt at him. She mercilessly slashed her talons through his dark plumage, satisfied to feel his warm blood on her claws. Then, she knocked him off his talons, causing him to hit the ground. Ellagard roughly pinned him, unable to care less if she sunk her talons into Khan's plumage.

Ellagard unleashed all of her suppressed anger, finally unable to hold it back for a second longer. "How could you be such a monster?" she screamed. "You ruined my life. Our lives!" Angry tears flowed from her eyes. "We were siblings once. We cared about one another. But you betrayed us all! And for what? Just some dumb dream you had about Jarquanzila!"

Something in Khan's amber eyes snapped. "I'm trying to help you! All of you!" Khan yelled. "You all call me evil. A monster. But look who just struck the first blow. Ellagard, for once in your life, stop trying to fight me. Just *listen* to me!"

Ellagard felt rage burn through her like a fire. "And why should I?" she spat. "You aren't a hero, Khan. Stop thinking that you are." She shook with emotion. "You murdered our own father, and countless others. You started the biggest war in the history of the tribes. You manipulated me! And now you honestly expect me to hear anything you have to say?"

Khan effortlessly threw her off of him, causing Ellagard to stumble backward by a few paces. "Yes, I do," he growled dangerously. "I am *sick* of this war. And I am *tired* of fighting all the time."

Khan extended his talons. "You will hear me," he demanded. "Because right now, you are the only one standing in my way of peace. Of finally ending Jarquanzila. And trust me, sister. I am not afraid to become the monster that you all call me."

Ellagard extended her own talons, feeling a rush of terror. There was no way that she could win a fight against Khan alone. So she would bide her time, desperately hoping that Reyna would arrive soon.

"Fine," Ellagard said. "What do you want, Khan? What was worth bringing me here alone?"

Khan's dark plumage smoothed slightly, but the deadly glint in his eyes remained. "All I want to do is talk," he began. "And, unlike you, I wasn't seeking a battle. So, let's have a conversation like the civilized leaders we are, shall we?"

Ellagard clenched her beak.

Khan began to slowly pace back and forth, his long tail feathers eerily flowing behind him. "Despite what the tribes gossip about me, I truly don't want to cause harm to you all," he said. "My fight has always been between me, and that snake Jarquanzila. And I *wish* that the tribes never had to get involved. If I could have left you all in peace, I would have." He stopped in front of Ellagard. "You and I both want the same thing, sister. An end to this war. Peace. So that got me thinking. Why should we both waste our time fighting against each other, when we both want to achieve the same goal?"

Khan dug his long, terrifying talons in and out of the earth underfoot. "I knew that it would be impossible to talk like this while in battle," he continued. "So I had no other choice but to use Zander, and my powers as a Speaker, to bring you here. I understand that what I did was cruel. And I'm sorry-"

"Get to the point, Khan," Ellagard interrupted, feeling impatient. "What do you want?"

Khan lifted his head, becoming even taller than before. "I want you to allow my rogues to peacefully enter the tribe," he announced. "We will destroy the Life Tree, without bringing harm to a single bird, and then we will leave." Khan smiled, looking genuinely happy. "After that, the war will be over. I will have no more reason to fight. And we can forget that this ever happened. Won't it be great, sister?"

Ellagard couldn't help but laugh, abruptly forgetting about her terror. Khan's smile slowly dropped. "You honestly expect me to just *give up*?" she mocked. "After all of this pain, after all of these years of suffering, you want me to surrender my tribe's Life Tree? Never." Feeling brave, Ellagard took a step forward. "You aren't just a monster, Khan. You're a joke!"

Khan recoiled, aghast. "But... but you were supposed to agree," he whispered in a hoarse voice. "This was going to be the end of the war. M-my redemption. My chance to move on." For the first time, Ellagard noticed how disarrayed Khan's dark plumage looked. How broken he seemed.

Khan looked down at his talons for a long, long moment. His eyes grew wide. "No," he choked out in a twisted voice. "No, no, no. I can't bear to be like this anymore. I can't bear to keep on fighting." Then, his hooded gaze creeped up to Ellagard. He laughed. And laughed some more. "So you want me to keep on being the villain, then?" he hissed. "Allow me show you just how villainous I can be!"

Before Ellagard even had a chance to react, Khan sprang at her. She felt her feathers get torn from out of her side. Then felt even more get torn out. Before Khan could land another blow, Ellagard rolled to the side, feeling her heart rapidly slam against her ribs. Khan swiped at thin air, then let out an annoyed screech. The dark peacock rounded on her, then pelted her with blow after blow from his powerful talons.

Ellagard quickly broke away, then slammed into his side with all of her might, hoping to send him reeling. But Khan only staggered backward by a pace or two. Fear struck Ellagard.

Khan repeated the same move as Ellagard, and this time she was sent tumbling halfway across the clearing. The breath was knocked out her chest, and she felt an explosion of pain. Khan slowly prowled toward her, his amber eyes glittering.

Ellagard struggled to her talons, but before she could even lift herself up, she felt a weight slam into her.

Khan pinned her with just a single talon, looking grim. "I tried to reason with you," he said. "I tried to end this peacefully. But I've gone too far. I was a fool to think that I could somehow redeem myself of all this chaos. So, from now on, I'll be even worse than all the rumours about me." Khan's eyes flashed with pain. "So long, Ellagard."

He lifted a talon high into the air.

Ellagard slammed her eyes shut, feeling nothing but horror. This was the end.

Then, a terrible screech tore through the silence. The weight was lifted off Ellagard. She opened her eyes, then let out a gasp. Khan was being driven backward, vicious blow after vicious blow. Ellagard couldn't believe it.

It was Reyna...

...and Zander.

The two peacocks continued to mercilessly attack Khan. The rogue let out a scream of disbelief. "What are you two doing?" Khan demanded, furious. "I am your leader!"

Reyna stopped dead in her tracks for a moment, casting Ellagard a dark look.

Ellagard felt her heart shatter into a million pieces. "No," she whispered. "Please, Reyna. Please tell me it isn't true. You aren't a rogue. Tell me you aren't a rogue!"

Before Reyna could answer, Khan sent Zander tumbling across the clearing, blood staining his talons. Reyna's eyes grew wide, and she immediately rushed to Zander's defense.

Just before Khan could land the finishing blow on the turquoise peacock, Reyna jumped onto Khan's back. The massive, scarred peacock's balance was thrown off. And, with a heavy thump, Khan collapsed. Reyna roughly slammed his shoulders into the ground, pinning him. Then, Reyna cruelly dug her talons into his plumage. Before Khan could throw her off, Zander rushed forward, adding as much weight as he could to Khan.

Khan's eyes grew wide. "Rogues!" he screamed as loudly as he could, his voice echoing throughout the hill of Misty Falls. "Help! Immediately!"

Reyna scoffed. "Oh, please. Don't be such a coward. It makes me embarrassed that I ever took orders from you," she mocked. Something in Reyna's voice was different now.

It was deeper, slyer, and more... natural.

Ellagard blinked at her in confusion. "Reyna, what do you mean, *orders*?" she weakly asked.

Reyna laughed. "Oh, Ellagard," she said coldly. "You really are a fool." Her yellow eyes slunk over to Zander. "You were right," Reyna told him. "She doesn't, and never did, have a clue. How... pathetic."

Ellagard froze.

Reyna smirked. "If it wasn't obvious already, my dear, let me just spell it out for you," she teased. "I used you. Plain as that." Her gaze lowered to Khan, and it turned cold. "This fool ordered me to pose as one of your tribemates. He wanted me to befriend you, and help lure you here when the time was right. With both Zander and I working together, you would be sure to come to Misty Falls eventually."

Reyna let out a soft *tisk*. "Little did Khan know that by pairing Zander and I together, he would have created the most fearsome duo in the history of the tribes," she said. "At first, however, I had nothing to do with this plan. It was only between Khan and Zander. But after Zander told me all about it, I saw an opportunity, and so did he." Reyna looked at Zander admiringly. "So, Zander convinced Khan to let me in on this little plan, completely unaware of our true intentions."

233

Zander nodded. "Khan made a deadly mistake to trust us," he added, grinning. "He was practically *begging* Reyna and I to betray him. And while he was dreaming up laughable plans for peace, we were making plans of our own."

By now, countless rogues had flooded the space, answering to Khan's cries for help. They froze when they spotted Khan buried beneath Reyna and Zander. Should they attack them? Or would they risk their leader's safety if they angered the two traitors?

Ellagard felt faint, realizing that she was completely surrounded. *I'm at the mercy of the entire pack of rogues,* she thought queasily. *Jarquanzila help me!*

Reyna looked pleased. "My fellow rogues," she began, her voice immediately silencing the crowd. "I know what you see before you may be... troubling. But Zander and I can assure you that everything is for a very good cause."

Reyna paused for a moment, commanding the attention of every peacock. Then, she lifted her head high. "Khan has betrayed all of us."

Reyna's words were met by gasps of disbelief.

Zander lifted a wing, signalling for silence. "Khan has brought the enemy, Ellagard, leader of the Peacock Tribe, right to our very base," he snarled, "with the intention of revealing all of our plans to her."

Khan let out a dangerous snarl, his tail feathers beginning to lash back and forth. "They are lying to you!" he screamed to his rogues. "What are you waiting for? Finish them off!"

Reyna and Zander looked smug as they watched the rogues exchange uncertain glances. No bird moved.

"Luckily, before Khan had a chance to betray us, we attacked him, as you can see," Reyna smoothly told them, as if nothing unusual had happened. "Khan is a liar, and a traitor. He must be punished."

Reyna's words were met by screams of agreement.

"Drive him away!"

"Tear his plumage off!"

"Feed him to the ocelots!"

Zander, eyes glowing with sick amusement, whispered something into Reyna's ear. The white birdess nodded, a grin sliding over her beak. Reyna turned to face the rogues. "Let's not get our talons messy dealing with something as lowly as a traitor," she said, voice slithering and cold. "What could be a better punishment than letting the once unstoppable leader of the dreaded rogues wander the jungle alone, with no place to go, and no birds to help him?" Reyna chuckled. "And besides, an ocelot will finish him off before morning, anyways. What a *depressing* fate."

Reyna and Zander stepped off of Khan. The dark peacock rose to his talons, eyes wide with disbelief. Khan waited for a long moment, hoping that some peacock would come to his defense. But, realizing that this wasn't going to happen, Khan took a step backward. And then another. Khan gave the rogues one last horrified look before turning his back and pushing past the crowd. He ran into the untamed jungle, soon becoming swallowed up by the dense green foliage.

Khan was gone.

Ellagard felt her blood turn to ice as Reyna's gaze slithered over to her. "Now, let's take care of you." Then, Reyna leapt at Ellagard with her talons dangerously extended.

# EPILOGUE

Cornelius drew in a deep breath, relishing the cool breeze as it danced around him. The sky above was clear, without a single cloud to dapple the bright blue. As Cornelius gazed out at the Blue Jay Tribe, he couldn't help but smile. Things were finally at peace. The SkyTalons had succeeded.

Blue jays were busily working all around Cornelius. They were clearing out broken twigs or uprooted bushes that had littered the camp during the battle with the seagulls. In a way, the blue jays saw this as a way to solidify how the old conflict was over. And, like the seagulls, the tribe was happy to move on and begin an even brighter future.

With all of this foliage gone, the camp now had even more space for the hatchlings to play, the Protectors to train, and the Healers to sort their supplies.

Cornelius released a heavy sigh. Although things were looking bright, not every problem had been solved. Myra was still out there, seething with hate and longing for revenge. And not every blue jay had returned to the tribe yet, after fleeing when the Shadow Within rose to power. Cornelius frowned. He remembered how a talonful of patrols had reported seeing traces of the missing blue jays outside of the tribe's borders. But, other than a few snagged feathers here and there, these blue jays had vanished without a trace.

*They might not even* want *to return,* Cornelius grimly thought. *They don't know that Dustin is friendly now. And the last they saw of the tribe, it was on the brink of destruction. I don't blame them for wanting to stay hidden. So, I hope that wherever these blue jays are now, they can be happy.*

The flap of wingbeats sounded behind Cornelius. He turned, then felt himself smile. Cornelius' two best friends, Shadow and Dustin, landed beside him. The two other SkyTalons sat on either side of Cornelius, and together the three birds watched the tribe thrive, peacefully silent.

Dustin, however, was much more silent than his friends. He kept his head low, and gaze dropped to the ground, like he always did these days. Cornelius saw this, feeling a flash of pity for his friend. Cornelius gently nudged Dustin, trying to encourage him. But all Dustin did was shift his head away from him even further.

Dustin had been reluctantly accepted back into the tribe, following the days after Jarquanzila had revived him. However, most of Dustin's tribemates had felt pressured into that choice. It was no secret that Dustin was not only the tribe's Speaker, but also the leader's hatchling. The tribe had been nervous to protest against a bird with that status, despite all of the terrible things that Dustin did.

It was clear to everyone that Dustin was no longer wanted. Birds didn't even try to stifle their gossiping whispers as Dustin trudged past them, keeping his gaze firmly planted to the ground. The only birds who really acknowledged Dustin anymore were Shadow, Cornelius, Atticus, and Elizabeth.

Now, Cornelius felt his heart twist. "What's wrong?" he asked Dustin. Although the small blue jay was usually in a grim mood, today he just seemed… different. Cornelius couldn't place his talon on it. "Are you okay?"

Dustin let out a heavy sigh. "No," he bluntly murmured. "I'm not okay." An awkwardly silent moment passed. Shadow and Cornelius exchanged a glance. Then, for the first time in a very long time, Dustin looked his friends in the eyes.

"There's something that I want to do," he told them, "but I won't go through with it unless you all agree that I should." Dustin hesitated for a moment, then spoke. "I want to leave the tribes… for good."

Shadow's eyes flashed with surprise. "What?" she exclaimed, shocked. Then, more gently she added, "but Dustin, you're a SkyTalon. The three of us need to stay together if we ever hope to defeat Khan."

Dustin stiffened. "That's my problem," he continued. "I don't *want* to defeat Khan. I know you all think badly of him, but when I felt like I was all alone, Khan comforted me. He supported me. He guided me to what I thought was right."

Dustin frowned. "I know that Jarquanzila proved he was good when he healed me. But, I still feel like Khan is telling the truth. I really do believe that he saw something off about Jarquanzila." Dustin shook his head, as if to clear a thought.

"Anyways, that's not the whole reason why I want to leave," Dustin continued. "Ever since I was accepted back into the tribe, everyone only ever sees me as a who I used to be. Not the bird that I want to become. And honestly, I don't think that I'll ever be able to escape my dark past. Not while confined to the tribes, at least."

Dustin looked at Shadow and Cornelius, desperate to make them understand. "That's why I want to leave," he said. "To start over. I want to create a new life for myself, where I won't have to be reminded of my mistakes."

Shadow frowned. "But then you'll be all alone," she said.

Dustin dropped his gaze, not wanting to show how unphased he was by that concept.

Cornelius gently placed a wing on Dustin's shoulder. "I understand why you want to leave," he told him. "We'll be okay on our own, if that's what you truly want to do. But know that to me, you'll always be a SkyTalon... and a friend."

Shadow reluctantly nodded. "The decision is ultimately yours, Dustin," she added. "But we will support you in whatever you choose to do. Never be afraid to follow your heart."

Shadow turned to look at the Life Tree. "But you must make your choice soon. Tonight, we will be leaving to begin our next mission: saving the Peacock Tribe. And we will go, with or without you."

Dustin nodded. "I understand," he told them. Holding back tears, Dustin hugged his friends with his wings. "Thank you for understanding. I knew that you would."


The moon's frosty, silver light beamed down onto the Life Tree island below. Atticus, Elizabeth, Dustin, Cornelius and Shadow stood silently, watching as the rest of the tribe gathered around. Not all of the blue jays could fit on the island, however, and many gazed out from across the lake, within the camp.

Soon after Dustin had revealed his plan to Shadow and Cornelius, he shared the news with Atticus and Elizabeth. At first, they had both been torn to know that Dustin wanted to leave the tribes. But, they quickly understood why, and gave Dustin their permission to do so.

Now, his father and aunt closely stood next to the small blue jay, looking grim.

After every bird had gathered, Dustin walked to the center of the crowd, keeping his head held high. But despite the confident movement, Cornelius could see nervousness glittering in Dustin's eyes. "Thank you all for gathering here tonight," the blue jay began, keeping his voice as steady as he could. "I know that you didn't come here because of me. But, before Shadow and Cornelius leave for the Peacock Tribe, there's something that I need you all to hear." Dustin paused for a long, long moment. "I won't be going with them."

Screams of protest tore through the night. "Traitor!" one blue jay screamed.

"Hey, hear him out!" Shadow yelled, silencing them.

Dustin looked at her gratefully, then continued. "I won't be staying within the tribe, either," he explained. "What I did to you all was horrible. I should never have taken my anger so far. And I understand why most of you will never forgive me." Dustin sighed. "So that's why I'm leaving. It isn't a secret that the tribe wants me gone. And I don't blame a single bird for thinking that. But just know that, before I go, I am truly sorry. And I always will be."

"But who will become our Speaker now?" Nathanial asked, perched high above in one of the Life Tree's branches.

Dustin winched. He hadn't thought of that before. His round eyes filled with concern, and they looked pleadingly at Shadow and Cornelius.

Then, a blue jay stepped forward. "I will," said Alessandra. Cornelius blinked at her, surprised. When they had found Alessandra just outside of the tribe's borders a few nights ago, it was as if she had become a completely different bird. In the days after Alessandra had returned to the tribe, Cornelius was shocked to find her much bolder and confident. Alessandra never hesitated to speak her mind anymore. *And I guess that includes her thoughts of wanting to become a Speaker.*

"I've never told anyone this before," Alessandra continued. "But I've always felt some sort of connection to the Life Tree. Even when I was younger. So, while the tribe is asleep, I often go as close to the island as I can to admire the tree. That's why Myra caught me all of those moons ago, and mistook me as a traitor who meant to harm it."

Dustin flinched, but Alessandra did a great job of ignoring him. "I don't have any training or experience as a Speaker," Alessandra admitted. "But I can't help but feel as if it is my destiny to become one. So, if the tribe and Atticus agree, I would be honoured to take on the position."

Alessandra's words were met by a chorus of approval from the tribe. Atticus nodded his agreement, his eyes distant. Cornelius could tell that the leader was thinking about his mate, and all of the pain the role of a Speaker caused him. But, in a way, Atticus looked relieved to finally be able to move on, and let a bird who actually wanted to be Speaker have the position.

Dustin's eyes sparkled with relief. Then, he turned to gaze up at the massive, open sky above. It was full of promise. Full of opportunity to finally be free of his pain, and to start a new life. One that he wanted.

Then, Dustin turned to look at Atticus and Elizabeth. They were the only family he had left, and he was about to leave them. Dustin opened his beak to speak, but he just couldn't find the words. So instead, he wrapped his wings around the two birds in turn. "We'll meet again," Dustin vowed, stepping back, "I promise."

Atticus forced himself to smile down at his son. "You better not get yourself into trouble out there," he joked. "Or else we'll be meeting sooner than you think." Atticus lifted a talon and patted Dustin's head, flattening his fluffy tuft of feathers. Dustin broke away, laughing as he fluffed it back up again.

Dustin went silent as he looked at Atticus and Elizabeth. Then, he turned to Shadow and Cornelius. "Goodbye," he whispered.

For the final time, Dustin gazed out at the tribe's camp in the distance. Then, with a massive leap, Dustin launched into the sky and flew off. Dustin eventually disappeared behind a cloud. The third SkyTalon was gone.

Cornelius stared at the spot where Dustin had vanished, failing at holding back his tears. *I probably won't ever see him again,* he realized. *But I'll never forget him.*

Shadow gently nudged Cornelius forward, toward the Life Tree. "Come on," she murmured. "It's time for us to go as well."

Then, the raven lifted her head to address the tribe. "Thank you all for everything," she began. "You have been kind to us. And we will never forget the adventure we shared, together. The times ahead of us are dark. We don't know what the future holds. But I promise you that Cornelius and I will stop Khan, once and for all. We will save the Peacock Tribe, and we will save all of you!"

Shadow's words were met by determined cries. As the tribe cheered the two SkyTalons on, Cornelius couldn't help but lift his head just a little bit higher. With Shadow by his side, he walked to the trunk of the Life Tree. This was it. The two SkyTalons were about to face their biggest challenge yet.

As Cornelius continued to walk, the colder the air began to become. He felt as though he was being plunged deeper and deeper into a frozen lake. The cheering tribe around him began to silence into nothingness, and soon the world went dark.

The SkyTalons had entered Jajarii.

"Shadow?" Cornelius nervously called out, unable to see her. His heartbeat quickened. Cornelius had forgotten just how dark Jajarii was.

"I'm here," came Shadow's voice.

Cornelius blindly stumbled to the direction of the call, letting out a sigh of relief when he caught sight of her silhouette.

"Keep on moving," Shadow told him. "Jarquanzila will take us to the Peacock Tribe in no time. Just think of where you want to go."

Cornelius nodded, even though Shadow probably couldn't see him. Then, he did as she asked. Cornelius, walking forward, fiercely thought about the Peacock Tribe. He refused to let any other thought slip into his head. *I can't mess this up,* Cornelius told himself.

Suddenly, Cornelius felt a tingle crawl down his spine. Something was wrong. For the first time, Cornelius realized that he couldn't hear the sound of Shadow breathing, like he had earlier. "Shadow?" he asked. No response. Cornelius desperately searched for her outline in the darkness. But Shadow was nowhere to be seen. Fear exploded through Cornelius. "Shadow!?" he screamed again.

Suddenly, a bloodcurdling screech tore through the silence. "Cornelius!" came Shadow's muffled, distant call. Then, the void was plunged into silence.

*Click... click... click...*

The sound of talons tapping against the ground began to approach. Cornelius felt his heart rapidly pound as the outline of a bird surfaced. The bird prowled closer. And closer. And even closer. Cornelius recoiled, feeling memories crash down onto him when he met the bird's eyes. "No," he whispered in a strained voice. "No. No. No!" Cornelius staggered, feeling the world sway from under his talons.

"Hello, SkyTalon," Aquila said, a smile creeping over her face. "I am so pleased to see you again at last. Now... let's talk."

## ABOUT THE AUTHOR

16-year-old Sophie Torro loves to write, especially about birds. At the

age of 11, she created a magical world of five bird tribes, and all the

dynamic characters that live within it.

Sophie currently lives in Canada, working on her future novels and

other exciting projects.